NOTHING BELONGS TO YOU

Also by Nathacha Appanah in English translation

The Last Brother
Tropic of Violence
Waiting for Tomorrow
The Sky Above the Roof

NATHACHA APPANAH was born in Mauritius in 1973. She was brought up there and worked as a journalist before moving to France in 1998. *The Last Brother*, her first novel to be translated into English, was awarded the FNAC Fiction Prize in 2007 in its French edition. Her novel *Tropic of Violence* won the Prix Femina des Lycéens in 2016, as well as seven other French literary awards.

JEFFREY ZUCKERMAN is a translator of French, including the Mauritian novelists Ananda Devi, Shenaz Patel and Carl de Souza. A graduate of Yale University, he has been a finalist for the PEN Translation Prize and the French-American Foundation Translation Prize, and a winner of the French Voices Grand Prize. In 2020 he was named a Chevalier in the Ordre des Arts et des Lettres by the French government.

Nathacha Appanah

NOTHING BELONGS
TO YOU

*Translated from the French
by Jeffrey Zuckerman*

MACLEHOSE PRESS
QUERCUS · LONDON

First published in the French language as *Rien ne t'appartient*
by Éditions Gallimard, Paris, in 2021
First published in Great Britain in 2023 by

MacLehose Press
an imprint of Quercus
Carmelite House
50, Victoria Embankment
London EC4Y 0DZ

A CIP catalogue record for this book is available
from the British Library.

ISBN (PB) 978 1 52942 283 2
ISBN (eBook) 978 1 52942 284 9

10 9 8 7 6 5 4 3 2 1

Designed and typeset in Warnock by CC Book Production
Printed and bound in Great Britain by Clays Ltd, Elcograf S.p.A.

MIX
Paper | Supporting
responsible forestry
FSC® C104740

Papers used by MacLehose Press are from well-managed forests and other responsible sources.

"And again and again, the heart – buried
deeply as ever in the human breast,
its four chambers exposed to love and joy
and pain and the small shafts that fall
with desperation in between."

Jamaica Kincaid, "At the Bottom of the River"

TARA

1

The boy's here. He's perched on the edge of the chair, his back straight, his body leaning forwards as if about to stand up. His face is turned to me and shadows flicker briefly across those incised features, I don't know where they come from or what they mean. I don't speak, I don't move, I shut my eyes but my stomach rumbles and the skin in the hollow of my throat starts quivering. It's the niggling fear the boy stirs up every time he appears, it's his silence, it's his stony presence, it's his way of looking at me, it's his ability to make me tremble, to knock me off-balance, it's because, even before I've laid eyes on him, I've sensed his presence.

When he's there, the air isn't the same, it's a shift in atmosphere as distinct as it's hushed, it turns cloudy and redolent of iron, wafting along my nape, down my arms, across my brow, my cheeks, my face. I sweat, my mouth goes dry. Nothing keeps me from curling up in a corner, locking my arms around my knees, dropping my head, and waiting for this to pass, but there's the odd feeling that I've experienced this moment a hundred times before. When, and where, I don't know, but I know this muggy breeze on my skin, this metallic scent, this sensation of having slipped outside time, and yet the way out has escaped me a hundred times over. Impatience rises up not unlike when I'm fumbling desperately for a specific word or someone's name; it's on my tongue, it's within reach, at my fingertips, it's so close. Then, even with my sudden fear and my flagging thoughts, I stop what I've been doing and go to find him.

It's not as if the boy's hiding or staying away, no, it's just as if he's found himself a cranny where he's waiting for me to happen upon him. One time he was at the back of the cinema, standing, the emergency-exit sign forming a red halo around his head. Another time, he was sitting on a bench in the park and, had his face not been turned my way, one would have thought he'd come to watch the passersby, the ducks and the way the trees' branches bent down to the water without ever touching. A week ago, I saw him standing in the rain across the street. His skin looked waxy and, even scared stiff, I felt an unexpected urge to kiss those shiny, wet lips.

And now, when I open my eyes again, he's still there, in the chair where I sit to read at night. It's the first time he's come to my place, I don't dwell on how he did it, if he sneaked in through a door that wasn't locked right, if he entered through the balcony, it doesn't matter, I know he's such a wily animal, creeping here, crawling there, appearing without a sound and disappearing as he pleases. If he felt like leaning back in the chair and stretching his left arm out, he could touch the spines on the bookshelf and hold the black egg-shaped pebble that's so smooth and perfect it almost seems manmade. I picked it up years ago on the beach at . . .

The beach at . . .

I don't remember the name. It started with an S. I can see it, this long strip of sand where, the day following a storm, the sea would leave behind bits of driftwood. I try to concentrate, I visualise the main street towards this beach, its uppermost, paved section, the shops dozing in the winter and staying open until midnight in the summer. In my mind, I go up and down this street, I try to trick my memory, to make it think I want to remember something different, that's how it works. There's an art to fooling oneself. So many details come back clearly: the painted wall of a shoe shop, the sugary smell of batter frying, the blue smoke of chicken being grilled on a makeshift plank, the stickiness of fingers holding an ice-cream cone, the roar of waves at night, the salt sprinkling downy arms and plump cheeks, but not the name of this beach. When the boy's there, there's a wall between particular words and me, between particular events and me, I try my best to reach them but it's as if they no longer exist. When the boy's there, I turn into a woman who trips over her words, who looks around, who gropes forwards, who stammers. My tongue is heavy, I make sounds like a baby, *sa, se, si*.

The quivering that started in my stomach spreads. I bury my face in my hands, clench them in fists over my mouth, and suddenly I remember Eli who should be here in less than an hour. I forget about the pebble, the beach, I look again at the boy who hasn't moved a centimetre.

He's wearing khakis and a short-sleeved shirt, its front pocket crimped by the metallic clip of a pen. His clothes are stiff, too big, straight out of the past, as if borrowed from his grandfather. On his feet are patent leather shoes that he's wearing without socks, like a dandy, but they're too big as well. From where I stand, he seems thin, skinny, maybe because of those oversized clothes. His face is a young man's – clear, deep-set features, heavy eyebrows, dark, thick hair – but the more I look at him, the more he strikes me as out of the past, faraway, someone who's traversed eras, memories, time.

His mouth shifts, maybe he's biting the inside of his cheeks, I know someone who does that, what's his name again? We worked in the same office for a few months, he had a long neck and liked to play solitaire at lunch . . . His first name starts with a D. *Da, de, di.*

The boy keeps looking at me intently but his gaze is neither hostile nor friendly. I wonder if he's reading my thoughts, if he can hear me straining to recall the name of that damn beach, that guy with a long neck, if he gets a kick out of being in my head, if it makes him happy to see me like this, shaking and at a loss for words. I search his face, his bearing, his stiffness, his waiting, for answers. Is it possible that he's growing more familiar the longer I look at him, as if he's blending, little by little, into the room's décor, as if absorbing the evening's tinge? Is it possible that it's not him I'm afraid of but what will emerge – now, soon, tonight?

Something along my spine pricks up when the boy's there, small jolts of electricity run up and down my back, and that, too, feels like something from the past, something I'd experienced long ago. My mind must be playing tricks, one second he's slipped away, the next he's back. I wish I could ask him what he's doing there, what he wants from me, why he's following me like this, why he doesn't say anything, how he appears and disappears, I wish I could tell him to leave. And I wish I could ask him his name.

I look out to the balcony, where the plants are drooping from three weeks of rain. *Tonight*, the radio host said, *it'll be nice out.* Then he clarified: *Tonight it won't rain.* The trees in the square visible from here are wizened. Everything's like that, in fact, after three weeks of non-stop, pounding, strident rain. Even the people look sickly, scared, bent over in fear of a downpour. Everything's slippery, crushed, washed away. Nothing stays. Only the water has any vigour, burbling through the gutters, swelling, flooding, hurtling, surging from somewhere unknown, from the very centre of the earth, no longer a molten core but a gushing spring.

The pearl-grey twilight has overflowed the outdoors and seeped inside. There's so much to do before Eli comes: shower, change clothes, get ready for him. This morning, he said on the phone: *I have to talk to you, can I stop by tonight?*

I know it's important. Eli's the sort to say what he has to say on the phone, it's his favourite possession, this thing he can pick up or hang up as he pleases, that he uses as armour or excuse, a call stands in for a visit, some distracted words for some time together.

I go through the doorway, I switch the light on, the grey scarpers off and the state of the room has me dumbfounded. Teacups and dirty plates on the low table, plastic bags lying about, clothes and blankets on the sofa. On the floor are books, magazines, papers, an overturned plant, mud. In my head, everything is swelling and shrinking. My thoughts all sink, now useless and waterlogged, and then, no, they resurface, they're still there. The sight of this room leaves me heavy-hearted and ashamed. It's so unlike me, I prefer everything in its place. I'm fond of every item in this house, I'd never leave a single one lying around like this. It's like a squatter's lived here. I can imagine the shock on Eli's face if he ever saw this. I wonder when it all began, was it the day the sky opened up over our heads, was it the day I first saw the boy, was it the day Emmanuel died?

I imagine Eli here, mouth agape, hands on hips, a habit he just can't kick. What would he be thinking about? About Emmanuel, his father, that wonderful man who married me more than fifteen years earlier and who died three months ago? About this event that made me a widow, him an orphan, and gave the two of us nothing whatsoever. It's easy to think losing this man would bring us closer in a way we never had been during his life. The love and respect and admiration we had for Emmanuel – emotions suddenly deprived of their object – might have coalesced, sublimated into affection, into some kinship that couldn't quite be labelled but that would endure in his memory, in our memories. But no. Eli has stayed distant, bound by no filial obligation, finally rid of me, and the sight of this room turned upside down leaves me with the unbearable thought that, tonight, he'll see me as a burden foisted on him by his father.

I look at the time, seven minutes past six, I've forgotten the boy in the armchair, I assess the situation as if starting on a maths problem. I take a deep breath, if I don't rush it, if I think calmly, I'll solve it. A long time ago, someone had told me how to work through maths problems, it was in an alcove, it smelled like cologne . . . it's a multifaceted memory that's coming back, glinting, shifting, hazy, I don't want it, not now. I need to stay focused. I have just an hour, no, let's say forty minutes, before Eli comes and I know what I need to do: bin bags, dishwasher, duster, vacuum, mop, fresh air. I can feel my brain working away, limbering up. I walk up to the window and the reflection shows me a woman in messy clothes but I look away quickly – I'll deal with that later. Ten past six. I say out loud, clearly, *You can't stay here.* I'm talking to the boy but not looking at him. Tonight, my words are aimed at the walls too, and the books, and the inanimate things in this room; they're aimed at these memories dragging me far from here, at this part of myself now rising up. Something stirs in the corner of my eye, is it him, is he going to stand up, is he going to talk to me, is he going to touch me, he can't touch me, I'll go to pieces if his skin so much as brushes against mine. I look him in the eyes and he fills my mind, the thought of Eli slipping away and escaping. I try to hang on to Emmanuel: he alone can keep me standing, intact, safe from my past life. But he doesn't exist anymore

This blanket rolled up on the sofa like a sleeping cat these plates with some scraps of food still there the cups the glasses the papers the magazines the clothes on the floor – they make me think of strewn puzzle pieces. I see them in greyscale like an old photograph, I don't understand them, why should I care, they're not my problem. I turn to the boy sitting in the armchair. There are books and magazines all around but I know he hasn't stepped on them or nudged them out of his way with those patent leather shoes. He's sitting feet together knees together, forearms on the armrests. I imagine him entering like a ballet dancer, whirling amid the swishing of his loose clothes, avoiding the books the magazines the piles of paper, setting first an arm on the chair's armrest, his body raised up and borne aloft by just this arm, then, in a fluid movement, tracing an arc with his legs and descending gently into the chair. As soon as he's landed firmly in the seat, he sticks his legs straight out and each one goes up and down slightly like two scissoring blades, then he tucks them in tight together and finally lets his feet ever so delicately touch the ground. I smile at the dancer boy because I, too, like to dance.

Arms folded over my chest, palms facing out, forefingers and thumbs of both hands meeting to form the almond shape of an eye, the other fingers out straight, feet and knees open. *Tat*, I extend an arm right as I stamp the right foot. *Tai*, I extend the other arm left as I stamp the left foot. *Taam*, I bring the two arms together. *Dith*, right arm forwards. *Tai*, left arm forwards. *Taam*, palms in front of my chest again. Again, a bit faster. *Tat tai taam dith tai taam*. I've already danced to these syllables, where they've come from or what they mean I don't know, but in front of the boy, they flow out of my mouth, pure honey. *Tat tai taam dith tai taam*. I recall firm pressure on my head so I would keep dancing lower, keep my legs bent, open, forming a diamond shape. With only a finger my elbows are adjusted so my arms stay even with my shoulders, with another my chin is raised. *Tat tai taam dith tai taam*.

The boy's bearing isn't quite so stiff now could it be I've danced for him before, could it be that's what he expects of me? The rhythm accelerates, I'm hot, I'd like to undress and dance with nothing on but bells strung around my ankles but I don't have any. Where are they? I need them on when I dance! I get down I crawl along the rug I lift up the magazines I'm sure they're under the sofa I can only get my hand under I have to lift this piece of furniture it's so heavy what's the point of being grown-up when I can't lift anything. My face is up against the seat. There's a familiar odour here I inhale deeply it reminds me of something it reminds me of someone who was there, who liked being there, someone I tried to lift as well and with that only that I remember, Emmanuel

My heart aches again. I should start by clearing the sofa, arranging the cushions, tossing a tartan rug over it, that'll be the first thing Eli sees, sentimental man that he is, inclined to believe that belongings gain a mysterious, almost human, aura in how they enter our possession, over the years or in connection to some particular moment. He's attached to things, a dried leaf, a pebble, an old toy, a yellowing book, a faded T-shirt, a broken wooden necklace that belonged to his mother, this sofa. It was on this sofa that his father died three months ago, and I can still smell it there, his scent, trapped in the cushions' fibres. It's not really the scent he had when he was alive but something that remains of him, that tugs at my heart, that brings me back to his absence and everything that's fallen apart since his death. Notes of vetiver, a touch of lemon, but also a trace of something powdery, slightly rancid.

I was the one to find him on this sofa. He was in the habit of coming in here to read. In his final year, he generally rose before dawn, he kept saying that he needed less and less sleep as he got older while I was the opposite, I always felt that as I shut my eyes at night I was living a different life, I was becoming someone else, and that neither my body nor my soul would ever rest. I could sleep until mid-morning and longer still, and yet I would never feel rested.

As I bury my head between the cushions, my thoughts close like a fist around the image of his large, round back and his bent knees, the bared soles of his feet. That morning, I had made coffee, I had toasted some bread, I had emptied the dishwasher, it was eleven o'clock already and I was thinking that he'd stir at the smell of coffee and toast, the sound of cutlery clinking on the table. He hadn't moved and I went over to him. All I want is to focus on that minute when I was watching him sleep, yes I was sure he was sleeping, I was saying his name gently, I set my hand on his waist, then brought it up to his shoulders and his hair which I stroked, such a soft down, and I still remember that feeling under my fingers, my alert, wary mind brings it all back, makes me feel it again. I was whispering, *Emmanuel.* He wasn't moving. I touched his brow and then noticed just how cold that brow was and with that I was shaking him, yelling his name and other things. That was when I tried to lift him up, my thoughts were of human beings carrying others, running, trying to save themselves or to save whoever they were carrying, they did that as if it were nothing and I thought I was strong enough to lift him up, bring him down the stairs, come out on the street and ask for help. But all I could do was drop him, pull him a few metres. My head in the cushions, my head trying to retain his scent, my head trying not to give out, my head wishing that the minute before my hand touched his cold brow, that moment could stretch out, expand, and become a bubble in which I could live the rest of my life. Just this lovely, innocent minute.

Eli asked me what I would do with the sofa. Nothing, I said, and he seemed relieved. Had he thought I meant to get rid of it? I stand up, I go and get a bin bag, throw in food scraps, packets of biscuits both empty and still sealed, tissues, newspapers, magazines. I gather up the books scattered all around, I'll shelve them later. I stack the plates and take them into the kitchen, I come back for the glasses and bowls and spoons. I don't linger over the mould, the rot, I put what I can in the dishwasher and start it. I don't know why the plants are on the chairs around the table, I put them back where they belong, I go and get the broom to sweep up the handfuls of dirt on the floor. I'm on my knees but something else rises up. A polished concrete floor that I sweep, wash, wipe dry. Hurry, hurry. Yes, a storm is brewing, the weather's shifting and a metallic odour's coming, I turn to the armchair. The boy is still there

The air is heavy, it's going to rain but hasn't it been raining for days and days this damp is weighing down on me, this feeling of trying to wriggle free, I swell the way doors swell in humid weather, my mind races, I have to sit down I push away the clothes the blanket this wool is bothering me, I pull off my cardigan my blouse I hike up my skirt to my thighs, what I wouldn't give for an ice-cold drink a fresh breeze the sea. I look at the boy sitting in the armchair, from here I wrinkle up my nose to sniff at his odour my mouth is a grimace but he doesn't smile and yet I know he's already smiled at this scrunched-up face I'm making too bad I raise my arms blow on my armpits my thighs I pull off my skirt quickly I blow between my thighs then I look at the boy. I know I've already gone through these motions, puckered my lips and blown on my skin to try to cool off. I'm sitting on an iron bed pushed against the wall I'm alone in a sheet-metal shed I hear crackling it's the ceiling bulb which is bare and emitting a yellowish light a dirty light a murky light and it makes me feel like I'm underwater. I see the front of my dress patterned with lots of small flowers fluttering because of how my heart is racing, and yet this fear is keeping me alive, this I'm sure of, it's a live wire running down my spine it's a state in which my whole body is tensed like I'm ready but for what I have no idea now. I've already faced up to this fear I know it's a mean dog I'm keeping by my feet and don't trust completely, maybe one morning the beast will turn on me, maybe go for my throat in my sleep, but for now the animal is there, sitting quietly, and if I keep calm if I keep doing exactly what I'm supposed to, soon there'll be a point when I've overcome this fear, when I'll be this dog's master forever. Suddenly in this room's cloudy yellow there's a movement in the corner the dog stirs fear spreads across my whole body I'm not alone anymore

What exactly I am – my self gasping in the nude on this floor and my brow dripping in sweat as if emerging from a long dream – what exactly I am now – my mind dozing and my person wrestling with this immense fatigue – what exactly I am – my body lying in a foetal position and my thoughts piling up in a jumble – I don't know. Maybe I could stay like this, until the day is wholly gone, until the night's inky darkness covers all? Maybe strength will return to my body, my senses will sharpen again? It won't rain tonight. It's nice on the floor, I could lie down for a while but I feel like I've forgotten something. It's in my head, floating somewhere with all those images, I can't make out whether they're the stuff of dreams or of memories. An armchair, a maths problem, an alcove, a dancing boy, an old shed, a bed, a yellow light. No, not something. Someone. Yes, that's it, I've forgotten someone. It was a long time ago, it was yesterday, it's now. I stay put, I've always been able to do that, anyone would think that I'd turned into a rock, but I'm just waiting, I'm breathing, I know that this thought will come to me eventually. If. I. Stay. Calm.

There. There. Here. Hush. Now. Yes. Eli. It's Eli.

Seven thirty-two. I try to get to my knees but I slip and bump my wrist. I put my weight on the other hand to get up, I reach for my clothes, what's happened here, what's got into me, here are the knickers to pull on, my legs are wobbly, here's the blouse to button up, I'm shaking, I grab the cardigan, no, I'm too hot I keep it in my hand, I fiddle with it, Eli's going to be here soon, I'm afraid he'll see the boy.

In the silent dusk, I keep my head down, it'd be nice to go into the bathroom, wash my face, do my hair, put on some lipstick, but I'm afraid of what might happen if I leave this room, if the smell of iron comes back, if I raise my head and realise that the boy is still there. I haven't cooked a thing, I don't know if I have anything to offer Eli, a bit of bread, some cheese or a glass of fruit juice, I don't remember when I last did my shopping. What will he think? How can I explain the state I've found myself in? I step back towards the sofa, there are still so many things to do before this room's presentable but I'm so exhausted. I decide to sit down and wait for Eli to come. I bury my face in my hands and I think: please make sure nothing happens, please make sure I keep my head make sure the boy goes and along with him this hot breath, this odour, this other soul who wants to dance in the nude, who's afraid, who hurts. It doesn't escape me that my words amount to a prayer. Maybe, when push comes to shove, even atheists like me end up hoping for some miracle to happen.

When Eli's here, in a minute or in ten minutes, I hope I'm brave enough, before he tells me what he has to tell me, to talk to him in a way I never have. I hope I can hold his two hands in mine and just say: when I get up, every day, I feel dizzy, I walk gingerly, both here and outside, I'm on the edge of a cliff. I feel like whole parts of my day play out without me, I think I'm losing my mind, it's the water, all this water, it's your father, it's the boy in the armchair, I don't know what he wants from me, come I'll show you.

2

Ever since Emmanuel died, Eli's always rung downstairs, through the intercom, and by the time he's got upstairs I already have the door of the flat open. He mumbles that he forgot his keys and I can almost believe he's done so to punish me, to get his revenge, like a little boy who's lost his father and sometimes has shameful dreams where I, his stepmother, am the one to die on the sofa. I can almost believe that he's acting like a landlord ringing at his tenant's place or that he wants me to know I'm nothing to him now, that he has no obligation, no connection to me anymore. But Eli isn't like that. Before, he ran up the steps, opened the red door, plopped his bag in the entrance, and shouted, *Papa, it's me!* How could he keep doing that when he knows his father's no longer there? I'm inclined to believe he uses the few minutes between when he buzzes and when he reaches the door to steel himself for this absence and for me, and me alone, to be living in the flat now.

Tonight, when he appears in the doorway, not having announced his arrival, I can't move. I try to smile but my face is overcome by spasms. He doesn't say hello, he looks around the room then stares at me, his eyes bulging.

"Tara? What's happened here?"

I glance at the armchair, the boy isn't there anymore. Eli slowly approaches me, one step after another, as if closing in on a skittish animal he needs not to scare off. He still has on his messenger bag, full to bursting with books and papers. Eli's recently become a secondary school maths teacher. I don't know how that's going for him, if he likes his work, what he does with his evenings. It was his father he confided in. We're only a few years apart but I feel so old beside him. So bound to the past.

Eli leans over to pick up something. It's my skirt. He repeats:

"What's happened here?"

"Nothing. I was tidying up."

"But . . . What's all this mess?"

"I was just tidying up. And then I felt tired."

"What's that smell? Something's rotting in here!"

I want him to calm down, to stop shouting with that shrill voice. I try to get up using my hands, rocking my body back and forth to stand up. No use. I shut my eyes, I imagine what Eli's seeing: the woman his father married more than fifteen years ago, this woman far younger than him, brought back from a devastated country and who doesn't talk much, a woman in underclothes with a rail-thin body, tan skin, a woman who's losing her mind, who forgets to wash herself, who's turned a nice flat into a dump, a woman who seems like she's a hundred years old and who can't even get up from the sofa. If I could muster just a bit of courage, I'd tell him that I'm still the woman who loves his father utterly, the woman whose sandwiches he likes, the woman who calls him at dawn on his birthday, the woman who's never wanted to replace his mother, the woman who stays awake when he's flying, the woman who tried to carry his father in her arms, the woman who understands just how immense and crushing Emmanuel's absence is.

My arms are utterly weak, utterly useless, it's like I'm a sick animal trying to stand. Then Eli comes over. His right hand grips my wrist, he slips an arm behind me, his left hand clasps my left elbow and he pulls me up. I look at him and, because some things never change, I know we're both thinking of the person no longer there. Eli's support is firm, he's so tall he can certainly see the top of my head, I collapse against him, I inhale the smell of cigarettes on his T-shirt. Without a word, he bends down and helps me step into my skirt. Did he ever imagine taking care of his father, did he ever see himself running errands, coming at weekends to handle odd jobs, taking him to appointments, those sorts of things without any fuss, any drama, any grief? Eli is bent down now, helping me to pull up my skirt, it's odd how there's no embarrassment and yet it's the first time we've ever been in such physical proximity. If only we knew where we stood in each other's eyes, then we could have spoken from those vantage points and used the words that are used when it's clear what one's role is: stepson, friend, big sister, stepmother. But our relationship has always been to Emmanuel and without him, now, we're just circling around one another. Eli touches my flabby, dry skin and helps

25

me bend my left leg, he looks at the slightly raised scar on the inside of my thigh. He says, *Papa's the one who sewed that up.* It's not a question, it's just words landing gently upon us and, for a few seconds, I let him look at this zigzag pattern without moving.

"Did you have your key today, Eli?"

"I was going to ring but I heard a yell. Did you yell?"

"No."

"I thought I recognised your voice. I was worried. After I got upstairs, I saw there was no garland on the door and then I started feeling scared. Did you not put one up this year?"

Oh, my dear Eli. Sometimes I forget how attached you are to these little things, a colour, a few words, a lilt, a bauble, and you do think that the hearts of those you love are to be found in those details. I really do admire your attachment, especially this evening, to these things that others would leave behind like so many skins that have been shed.

Every New Year's Day, I hang a garland of fresh mango leaves up on the door. I go and buy them by the train station, in an Indian shop, and on New Year's Eve, I tie the leaves' stalks to a cotton cord and right before midnight I hang the garland. I explain that it's to bless this home, to bring luck to those living there, to ward off grief, but I say that because I know how much people here like such sweet little exotic traditions. When he was living with us, Eli was the one who hung up the garland and I held the stepladder steady. Emmanuel teased me, saying that there was never any risk Eli might fall from that sturdy stepladder while I pointed out that Eli wasn't complaining. For those few minutes, as the smell of

26

mango-tree sap surrounded us, I felt like Eli was waiting for me to share a memory that would be mine alone, that would be from my heart and from where I was born. No stories about natural disasters or conflicts but words much like a folktale or a lullaby. It was a sort of bubble we were in each year, for a few minutes – Eli hanging the garland and waiting for me to share; me uselessly holding the stepladder steady and never granting Eli what he was waiting for because I was well aware of what misfortunes lay behind the veil of stories and songs. As the years went by, did he grow disappointed by my useless babble, did he see through my attempts not to remember, not to share? Once he was down again, I always told him, never daring to touch him, *Yes, it's perfect like that, Eli.* He smiled at me and the line separating the two of us, the one he'd drawn in the sand the day I'd entered his life, reappeared. It wasn't indifference towards me, no, not so much as a respectable distance. Maybe it's also a defensive reaction he has upon seeing his father's wife and I'd always respected that line.

"I didn't want to do it this year without your father. I'll put one up next year."

"I can hang it up, if you want."

Could it be that some part of me has stepped across the line in the sand, has breached this polite distance? Could it be that, when we're not looking, the heart puts out its vines and goes on longing, loving, pining?

"Do you want something to eat?"

"No, Tara. Stay here, I have to talk to you about something."

Eli sets me down on the sofa and, rather than sit beside me, starts tidying the room. He opens the windows and the fresh night air rushes in, driving out the odours. He gathers, throws, empties, tidies, sweeps, washes, dries. Every so often he glances at me but I don't say anything, I smile, I watch him take charge. My face softens at the sight of the flat reappearing little by little. My heart is light, as if nothing is tugging at it, nothing is crushing it. Eli makes several trips to the rubbish bins, I didn't realise there was so much to throw out. I look at the armchair, the boy's come back but he doesn't scare me anymore. I've recognised him. I lie down. I shut my eyes.

3

Hunger finds me in a dream where I walk barefoot through a field. Everything here is more intense – the colours, the textures, the sensations. It's a well-tended-to plot with clusters of long, thin leaves poking up at regular intervals. In this dream, I know I'm both myself and someone else – someone who knows the name of these leaves, who knows that they're ready to be harvested and who's careful not to trample them. Someone light-hearted. I like being her, I like being in her body and mind, our feet sink into cool, thin mud, it's sensual, pleasant, it squelches between our toes. At the end of this flooded field, there's a wood and at the edge of the wood I make out silhouettes that seem to be draped in loose clothing billowing and fluttering in the wind. I don't know what they're doing, it doesn't matter, we're not afraid of them. I'm in a *tableau vivant* that starts and stops here, everything's there, the past, the present, the future, everything is contained in this field flecked with green, in this airy mud under a rounded, blue sky. I'd like to stay here forever but, in this dream, just as this someone else knows the names of these plants, she knows to steer clear of the water snakes fond of coiling around the base of these plants, so we hurry on, hopping between the clusters, this way and that, and I laugh, I laugh! When hunger finds me and pries me out of this dream, she's running towards a house, her heart filled with all the impishness of a beloved child.

On the sofa, I keep my eyes shut in hopes of falling back asleep and being drawn back into this dream where the greenery is still there. I can't, my starving body refuses to doze. Immense sadness overcomes me, born out of nostalgia for both the immense beauty of this dream and the wellbeing I felt, and out of regret as I know what will become of this girl, I know just how brutally her childhood will be ended. I know her, this girl, I don't want to say her name, not now, not yet, it's been so long since I've dreamed of her, since I've thought about her like that, bounding barefoot through a rice field, when all was calm, when all was sweet. I keep my eyes firmly shut, I feel like that's the only way I'm able to think of her, when I can't see anything around me. She's both present and past, frozen in her joy and her bounding, still innocent. This way, I can believe she's made of the same stuff as an ordinary dream and forget her.

But ever since Emmanuel died, it hasn't been enough for this girl to live in my dreams. She's growing inside me, pushing against my ribs, she wants to get out and I can tell that soon I won't be strong enough to hold her in any longer, she's that haunting, that powerful. She's the one who sent the boy, the one who makes me forget words, occurrences, she's the one making me dance in the nude.

My stomach lets out louder and louder groans, I shift slightly on the sofa, bend my legs and straighten them. I open my eyes, I stand up. I plant my feet on the rug. I wait but nothing comes: no dizziness, no feeling of suffocation. For the first time in ages, I feel relaxed, a weight has lifted off my chest, and I'm no longer afraid. Was it those hours full of sleep, crammed with iridescent dreams? Was it Eli's presence yesterday or just now or some time I can't be sure of anymore? I remember the comfort of seeing him busy himself like that, gathering, washing. Where is he? What time could it be?

"Are you awake?"

"Oh! You scared me!"

Eli's voice is that of someone who hasn't been sleeping, who has just been waiting.

"Sorry. How are you feeling?"

"Good, good. Really. I haven't slept like that in ages. What time is it?"

"A bit past three in the morning."

"Oh. It's early."

I don't turn to him. I let his gaze float in front of me, somewhere on the rug. Eli's sitting in the armchair, where the boy was just before. I stand up.

"Where are you going?"

"Into the kitchen, I'm hungry."

"Tara, no. Stay here, I'll bring you something."

In the darkness, Eli heads to the kitchen. A ray of yellow light falls across the doorway. I hear him rummaging in the refrigerator, opening the cabinets. I'm not sure what to think anymore. Eli's voice worries me, it hints at something held back, trembling, about to burst. I wish he'd leave, actually. All I want is to eat, go back to sleep, and wake up late in the morning, under a bright sun. It won't be humid anymore, there won't be rank breath on my neck anymore, there won't be dizziness anymore. I'll be able to hang on for a few more weeks.

Eli reappears and says:

"Just so you know, I'm going to switch on the light."

"No, please, not the ceiling light. The lamp there, on the left, that'll be nice."

He obeys and light pools on the now-empty armchair. I wonder: if I squint and stare at that, might I make out the outlines of a being from the past dressed in clothes too big for him? Eli returns with a tray that he sets on the coffee table. It holds biscuits, chocolate, almonds, water, two plates, a roll of paper towels. I shift over on the sofa and he sits down beside me. Wordlessly, he takes a plate, fills it with a bit of everything, and hands it to me. He does the same for himself and I notice that our movements are fluid, even graceful, as if we're dancing underwater. We eat and drink in silence. But it's a truce. I know Eli's getting ready, I can almost hear him thinking, struggling with himself, making up his mind then changing it. My dear Eli, let's let the dead rest, I suddenly feel an urge to say, leaning my head on his shoulder.

Then, once our plates are empty and carefully stacked and, to my surprise, there's no awkwardness between us, I start hoping that Eli won't say anything, that he'll go and I can lie down right here and wait for day to break. Will he grant me this respite?

But Eli starts talking. It's like he's telling a story and even though he's talking about me in this story, my mind is flitting like an insect. Landing here, taking off, disappearing, returning. He starts thus: *I came to see if everything was alright because you haven't been to work for several days. Pascal Gress called me, he told me that you'd been seen in town dressed all in white. That sometimes you left the office without any warning.* Pascal is the doctor who's taken over the practice and he's kept me on in the administrative assistant job I had when Emmanuel was alive.

Eli says things about the evening before, I catch, "I didn't recognise you," "I was afraid," "It smelled terrible," "It was filthy." He keeps saying, "I don't understand," "I'm sorry," "You're so thin," "I feel bad." When I don't hear him, I think of my dream. It was so beautiful, so clear, with not one shadow. That's a sign, a warning. Suddenly it seems like Eli's talking about my bedroom and I turn to him. His face is grey, leathery.

"You went into my bedroom?"

"To get a blanket. You'd fallen asleep on the sofa and I didn't want you to be cold."

"Did you touch anything?"

"No. I just took the blanket."

Eli's lying. I've observed him for years. His mouth twists to the left, something that could be mistaken for a sly smile. Tonight, his head's bent slightly, his hands together between his knees, and I recognise this tic of his, it's a thread that tugs at the left corner of his mouth, once twice three times.

Deep calm falls over me, I think back to my dream and I can see that it's the beginning of the end for me. There's no point struggling, fighting it off. I think I've known that since

Emmanuel died but I'm just delaying the inevitable. I look at the armchair, I'm surprised to see it empty.

"You never talk about yourself, Tara."

"About myself? What do you mean? I don't understand."

"You cut your hair, I didn't notice last time."

"Mm-hmm. Yes, I did, a few days ago."

"Papa told me how you met."

I want him to stop right there, I don't want to talk about that, but it's too late, the boy's come for me, I know it now. Could it be that, all this time I thought he'd abandoned me, he's been out looking for me?

"I don't have it in me to talk about Emmanuel tonight. I'm sorry, Eli."

"Who is Vijaya?"

That name lands like a slap. It doesn't knock me flat, though. On the contrary, it wakes me up, it shakes me out of this illusion I've been under for three months, this fantasy that I'm strong enough to resist the onrush, the wave, the mean dog. Emmanuel isn't here to shield me anymore and, now that he's gone, so is Tara.

"She's nobody."

My back is straight, like when I was in the shed waiting for the boy, but Eli's as reserved as his father. He doesn't press the matter. I hear him say, *Don't worry about it*, and he, hardly ever one to touch me, sets his hand on my knee.

"We have an appointment at the hospital tomorrow."

"Tomorrow?"

"At eleven. While you were sleeping, I called Pascal, who referred me to a neurologist, and we set it all up."

"A neurologist?"

"Tara, I think it's important for you to see one. Look at yourself, you're not doing well. They'll do a few tests, maybe you'll stay at the hospital for a day or two."

"Tests?"

"To get the full picture, see what's not working."

"What's not working?"

"Yes."

I try to stay calm but I can't go to the hospital, I can't answer their questions, I can't let them dig through my head. I imagine them prying out my memories and showing them to Eli one by one. I can't let that happen. Those are things that belong to me, me alone, now and always.

I lay my own hand on Eli's and this time his smile is genuine.

"Is that alright?"

"Yes, Eli."

He exhales loudly as if he's been underwater the whole time he's been talking to me. He looks at his watch, nods, looks at the armchair then me, he shifts his legs and that, too, I know well. Each time he's come to see me, he seems to arrive with a specific set of lines to say and after he's run through them all, he doesn't know what to do with his hands, his head, his body. All he wants is to leave, and so he gets up, acting like he's having a stretch. He's so predictable that I have to smile.

"You can go home, Eli."

"No, no, I'm going to stay and tomorrow I'll take you to the hospital."

"Eli, you can go home and come and pick me up tomorrow."

"No, I can't leave you here."

"Whatever you want."

I slump back on the sofa.

"Are you going to sleep here, Tara?"

"Yes."

"On the sofa?"

"Mm-hmm. You can lie down in your room, your bed's made."

I know Eli won't go into his room, he hasn't been able to bear this flat ever since his father died, he can barely breathe, his father may be nowhere but his father is everywhere.

He takes the tray. I hear him doing the dishes, putting the clean plates away and, as I knew he would, he comes back to tell me that he'll go and get his car which is parked some distance away and head home for a few hours.

"I'm going to rest for a bit, take a shower, and tomorrow, at ten fifteen, I'll ring downstairs."

"No, use your key, please. I'll be waiting for you."

"Alright. I'll call you before I head over, if you want, so you're ready."

"See you tomorrow, Eli."

"No, see you soon. It's four in the morning!"

We have a laugh, a quiet, polite *ha ha ha* like two strangers nodding to one another on a bus. Eli walks over, pulls the blanket up to my shoulders. I shut my eyes, whisper a *thank you*. I can feel him close by, he's looking at me, this woman who's lost her mind, and after a few seconds, he leans down and kisses me on the cheek. When he leaves, I cup my hand over it, I imagine holding in this kindness, a little longer, just a little longer, and for a few blessed minutes, that's all that matters.

After that, I get up and go into my bedroom. I knew Eli was lying: he's gone through the rubbish. All the crumpled papers have been smoothed out, he's cleaned the ashes off the desk. I have to act before the boy comes back, while my mind's clear. It's time to put a stop to it all.

4

I'm sitting on the edge of my bed, I'm not moving, I'm waiting
for something unknown, maybe a signal, some noise outside, a
voice in my head, but nothing comes apart from the outlines
of what's around me, it reminds me of a soft darkness from
a long time ago. I'm not sad, I'm not unsure, I'm not afraid
anymore, I'm just a seated figure, leaning forwards, waiting for
something unknown. Oh, it's coming from my stomach, it's
like a rubber band pulled tight and now, suddenly, snapping,
I jump up and this is what I do before dying.

First I pull down all the bits of paper covering the stretch
of wall in front of me. My eyes run over the handwriting,
chicken scratch, calligraphy, emphasised with block letters or
in red marker. "My name is Tara," they all say. I throw them
out. On other sheets that Eli pulled out of the bin, the name is
crossed out. "My name is T̶a̶r̶a̶ Vijaya." I open the desk drawer
and confetti spills out: papers with X'd-out names that look
like a madwoman's scribbling. I empty it all out immediately.

I pull nice sheets out of the wardrobe and make my bed.
I smooth them out several times with the palm of my hand

so there isn't a single crease. I have a sense of déjà-vu – I've emptied out my desk and taken the papers off the wall before, I've made my bed like this before – perhaps this isn't the first time I've gone down this road, perhaps I've tried to end things before? What kept me from following through?

Tonight, I'm determined not to let myself be moved or distracted. I just need to think of Eli who saw these papers, I just need to imagine the appointment scheduled with the neurologist. It's too late now to think I can avoid the inevitable.

I work quickly, efficiently. I go through the flat without letting myself linger on anything – not that photograph, not that book, not that CD, not that memento – all these things that, just a few months ago, when Emmanuel was alive and kept me whole, seemed to be part of me, and I of them. I visualise what's next, my mind doesn't waver, it's focused on a specific outcome. It's been ages since I've been so unwavering but I don't let myself be fooled, this is an illusory state, even a treacherous one. Just one gust of humid air will bring me crashing down.

I come back and sit at my desk to write to Eli because that's what people do in these situations. They leave a note, a letter, something to console, if not to explain. Where should I start? I keep thinking of lazy truisms, "I love your father," "I care about you," "I miss Emmanuel so much," "the grief is unbearable," "I want you to have a happy life," and "sorry" over and over. But I can't seem to get to the raw truth of this moment in which I'm not truly Tara anymore and not Vijaya yet. After an hour, I decide not to bother with this final kindness. I stick my hand in the bin, rummage through the heap of papers as if drawing

lots, the winner is a Post-it note, a yellow square. I flatten it
out, stick it carefully to my desk, and look at it.

My name is Tara

An image of Eli at this desk, reading this yellow paper,
suddenly comes to mind and, before this image summons
another and then another, I get up, I grab the bin, and I step
out onto the balcony. It's not raining anymore but the air
still seems sodden after these interminable days of torrential downpours. I imagine my hair getting frizzy, the doors
swelling and sticking in their frames, I can see the little star-
bursts speckling the bathroom wall, the photo magnets on the
fridge with their peeling corners, I recall the smell of clothes
not fully dry. How clearly all this is coming back! It would be
easy to give up, here, now, barefoot on the balcony. It'd be so
easy to cling to this belief, to trust my body and my mind just
a little longer. I listen to the new silence across the city and
wonder how many days of sun it will take for everything that
swelled, contorted, got dirty to return to its original state. I
burn everything there is in the bin and, every so often, I watch
a sheet catch fire between my finger and my thumb, then I let
it go into the waning night.

I take a long, practically scalding shower, I want to stay
awake, I want to stay in control to the end, but as I get dressed
I wonder why I bothered to shower because this is the end and,
at that thought, my eyes fill with tears. I think of my dream
and everything it contained – rice fields, joy, innocence. I'd
have liked to stay in it and see my father, my mother. Through
the window, I see that the edge of the sky is brightening and I
say, as if speaking to someone in the room, beside me, *We need*

to go now! My voice echoes and bounces off every inanimate thing here, bounces against my body.

In the entrance, my head is bent over the old piece of furniture as I check the zipper pocket of my fleece jacket for my ID. I'm not scared of imagining my body mangled, twisted, a formless mass, but I do hope this plastic card will stay intact. I don't want to be anonymous, just another dead body, no, I want to be found, identified, declared dead. I grab my keys and, at the whitewashed chest of drawers, I resist the urge to look at myself in the mirror the way I always do before leaving the flat. It's a compulsion that comes from deep in my core, seizes my neck, makes me raise my head.

With a movement not unlike retching, I finally leave but right before I do, I glimpse my reflection one last time and I can't let go of it as I hurtle down the stairs, pull out my bike, pedal through the turtledove-grey city to the river. What I saw and cannot forget is a face with murky contours, features erased partway. My heart pounds as I wonder, leaving my bike by a tree, who this half-seen presence was: Tara? Vijaya?

The turbid, muddy river is in spate, churning with strong currents. I head up the bank, going around the houses there. I think some have been evacuated. Did those who stayed watch the waters rise, hour by hour, the same way I, ever since Emmanuel died, have been watching this incursion into my body and my mind? Will they ever give up in the face of this influx threatening to destroy everything, or will they still be there tomorrow, stacking more sandbags, hauling furniture upstairs, hoping? Will they set off with packed suitcases or empty hands?

I leave the residential area, drawn to the endpoint I've chosen, and soon find the walking path. Crystal-clear day is here now. The trees are taller, leafier than I remember, in some spots they form a bower over the path, and the space becomes a halo of green. I walk through this hue as if into a liquid landscape, maybe this is what's become of the air after all these torrential days, maybe my mind's wandering again, in any case it's nice to be buoyed by this feeling for a few minutes more.

The path runs along the old train tracks and I notice that the wooden railway ties are crumbling, almost covered in moss now. *Soon*, I keep repeating to myself. Soon the final ascent. Soon, up there to the left, I'll be able to make out the iron beams of the old railway bridge. Soon, I'll be on the bridge. I've come here so many times, by bike, on foot, with Eli, with Emmanuel. I often sat right on the span to catch my breath, I sometimes traded a few words with passersby. In the summer, I even went down to the riverbank and lingered under the weeping willow because I do like those trees that seem right out of a bedtime story. I wonder what goes through people's heads when they make such plans, what emotions and memories and reasons emerge to determine the how and the where. As for me, I thought of the bridge right away – how could I not?

Suddenly, up on the hill, there's a dog. In the morning light, it's yellow. I stop in my tracks. Two other dogs appear, unmoving, perhaps standing guard. Then I make out a silhouette and the group starts moving again. My heart pounds, as long as they're coming I can't go. It's a young woman with three dogs, that's nothing, just a woman with three dogs, but I get the impression they don't see me. Like I don't exist. Could it be I'm already gone? Could it be just the thought is enough for me to actually disappear? I notice her hair – earth-toned dreadlocks down to her waist – and her camo jacket and her cargo trousers. She's rather young in fact, barely out of her teens. She's got a big backpack with three lunchboxes hanging off it and clanking against one another at every step. The dogs aren't on a leash but stay close to her like bodyguards. They're thin, short-haired, with the occasional straw-coloured tuft, I can see them better now. And then I'm reminded of those dogs that prowled around me when I was living in the refuge for girls – they were like these ones, like prehistoric animals.

I watch them move further off, my heart racing, and when they reach the bottom of the hill, the dogs are still moving as they turn their heads to me in a single smooth movement and the horrifying thought comes that they're the same animals, sent by someone unknown, from my past, that they've recognised me, that they've seen right through me. First the boy, now the dogs!

I start running but my legs are leaden, my body feels stuck in thick mud. I advance a centimetre at a time, the air that just a minute ago seemed so fluid and gentle is now so dense around my head and my shoulders as to make my knees buckle. My left leg is heavy, my scar is throbbing, as if it were about to burst open. I can see the bridge at last.

Is that what impending death is – this sensation of coming apart, of seeing a body drag itself out of me, press on, unafraid, unburdened, unaged, actually running, scaling the metal lattice, hoisting itself onto the highest bar and standing there, teetering above the water and the woods and myself? Which of us is standing, which of us is on the ground?

I barely make it to where the span begins, my breath akin to a groan, my belly clenching and inflating again, I'm sobbing, my ears are ringing and I feel like I could just collapse here, so close to the end, so close to my dying wish, I can feel the warm humid breath of failure. They'll find me, they'll drag me back, and I'll be forced to live, to go to the hospital, and to endure both forgetfulness returning and deep-buried memory resurfacing. I'll be forced to tell Eli the truth and that prospect is unbearable. I'd like for his image of me to remain that of a woman who was discreet, loving, and loved, who, upon her husband's death, lost her mind. A woman of few words but deep affection for him. I'd like for him to remember that my name was Tara.

Through the bars of the bridge, I can see the churning waters, it's high enough that I can touch them from here. Then I hear the dogs barking. They're getting close, their yaps fill the air rinsed by all this rain and the young woman must be close behind.

I remember everything, it rises in me like an urge to vomit, it wrenches my guts and threatens to pour out here in thick black clumps in this spot where I am at peace. I remember that the name my father gave me meant "victory". *Vijaya.* I stand up, I look at the tightly woven metal lattice and I know I don't have the time or the strength to climb it. The dogs are here, the young woman's yelling, *Stop!* The unexpected, sweet thought comes that she's suddenly talking to me like she's known me forever, but why should I care, I want everything to die with me: the boy, Tara, Vijaya. I drag myself to the riverbank that doesn't exist now because the water's so high, because the current's overrun the earth, flattened the vegetation. I try to stand up but there's nothing under my feet. My body gives out. I'm shocked to be yelling like it's a surprise, as if there's still a tiny part of myself refusing this act and I want to rip out that part, grip it in my hand, look right at it, listen to it tell its story, but then

the water,

all this water

VIJAYA

5

For a long time I believed the life I led would never change.

It was a life of deliciousness: mangoes, coconut water, steaming rice, red curry, fried fish, yoghurt, honey, thick spongy fritters, fresh milk, ice cream made from that fresh milk's cream and cardamom pods, pickled cucumbers, caramelised bitter gourd. I liked sweet, sour, bitter, salty, mouth-puckering; I liked raw and cooked; I liked green and ripe; I liked crunchy and soft. My parents said I had very grown-up tastes, they smiled at how enthusiastic, how curious I was to try new things. Was it possible that I already knew, deep down, that it wouldn't last? When my father went to the capital, he brought back creamy pink biscuits imported from abroad, sweets and fizzy drinks, but I liked Aya's cooking more. Aya had always lived with us. The kitchen was where she reigned and, whenever I saw her anywhere else, she struck me as so frail, so fragile. I had her try those biscuits and she said exactly what I thought, *It's like wet sand.* There were a few pink crumbs on her chin. I blew to get rid of them.

It was a life of warmth: my mother's hand on my cheek to

wake me up, her way of saying, *Yes, Vivi,* when I asked her something, the American songs she listened to in the morning on her radio cassette player, the warm water poured over my shoulders, the soap that lathered into a white foam on my body, the oil rubbed into my hair, the kisses my father planted on my forehead, the way Aya called me *kutti,* meaning "little" in her language. *See what I made you today, kutti.* The moonless nights when my parents and I, lying on the grass, looked at the sky full of stars, and we named the constellations. I wanted those nights to last and last. I clutched my parents' hands. I pulled them tight, I pulled them to my chest. There, that felt nice. I could stay that way forever and ever.

It was a life of freedom: I went everywhere barefoot, I jumped into the pond anytime the lotus roots and frogs were cleared out, I climbed up trees, I walked on the edge of the well when nobody was watching, I dangled from the beams over the veranda, I ran through the rice field and its cool mud while sidestepping the shoots and, even when I heard Aya in the distance calling me, *Kutti, come home!,* I kept on going this way and that, with this feeling that my mind and my body were one and that any second now I could fly.

It was a life of busyness: at seven o'clock on the dot, from Monday to Friday, I went into my father's office and headed to an alcove on the left that was what we called school. In there were a chair, a desk, a board, colourful posters on the wall, a world map, books, notebooks, pens and pencils, card games, puzzles, a radio. My father was always waiting for me, stony-faced, his warm smile gone, his hands behind his back, and, in this room that smelled like wood and rubber, for five hours, I had to call him Mister. There was so much to learn, so much to remember: maths, languages, history, geography, physics . . . all those things that he himself had learned when he was my age and going to a colonial school thirty years before. Mister didn't believe in the education given at the independent schools of this independent country. Some evenings, I heard him and his friends complaining about the mediocre education here, our leaders' narrow-mindedness, and he used words I didn't know, that I tried to remember so I could ask him what they meant but I forgot them too soon. He was always saying *before, before, before.* He said that those schools were sending this country back to the stone age. If he caught me daydreaming, if my work wasn't done right, if I complained to my mother about homework, if I dragged my feet, if I ate a snack behind his back, Mister threatened to send me to the village school. Down there, he said, there's no homework, no poems to memorise, no languages to learn, no maths problems, and no world history. Down there, I'd only speak one language – the one the leaders wanted to force on us as the official language, the one they said was better than all the others. I knew it was Aya's language. I knew that was the language she hummed in. I liked saying some words in it by calling up her language in my mouth, keeping my lips half-parted as I wrapped my tongue around the sounds. For all the love and reverence I felt for my father, I couldn't help but find this language beautiful, although I never told him so. Mister informed me that, in that school, I'd learn only the history and geography of this country. Every morning, dressed in strict uniform like a little soldier, in rows with dozens of other little girls, I'd have to sing a song to the glory of this country in front of a raised flag. Down there, he added, the teachers walk with a thin bamboo rod and, should I be unlucky enough to forget any words to that song, *thwack!*, they'd whip the branch across my calves.

Once he'd finished telling me all this, Mister asked me if I wanted to go to that school and I imagined my mind stunted and wilted like that old pea I'd once found in the kitchen. I thought of the fiery bite of that branch on my legs and I was quick to shake my head. The hardest part, though, was when Mister sat beside me and I could smell his cologne. That scent swept away the teacher, brought back my father, and in an odd optical illusion, the man began to blink in and out, a smiling father one moment and a strict teacher the next. At those times I was struck by the lack of other children my age, who were off in a classroom practically out of the Stone Age, and of a father I could call Papa all the time.

On Tuesdays and Thursdays, Rada took the train from the capital to come and teach me Bharatanatyam. After lunch, I waited on the top step of the veranda. I'd draped my special sari the way she'd taught me to; my mother had oiled my hair and braided it in a long plait. Beside me my ankle bells had been set down. I crooked the fingers of my right hand and, through what I thought of as a telescope, I watched the spot beyond the rice fields where the dirt path through the small woods between us and the village began. Apparently one's sight can get blurry when one keeps staring at a point, but I had the impression that the longer I watched that spot, the more the details grew distinct. The grooves on the tree trunks, the different shades of green on the leaves, the way they fluttered in the wind. I didn't want to miss when her tuk-tuk came. There was no way to know what colour her taxi would be, and when the red or yellow or green or orange speck appeared in the telescope formed by my fingers, I stood up and couldn't keep myself from waving as if I were a castaway trying to catch a rescuer's attention. I had no idea whether she could see me but I only stopped once her tuk-tuk had deposited her in front of our gate and Roy, the gardener, was already there, fiddling with the padlock. Roy smelled like standing water and had only one eye, but I'd never been scared of looking directly at him – my mother had taught me to meet his right eye, the good one, the open one, the one that always seemed to be a bit teary, full of goodwill, even if sometimes a shadow flickered across it. I didn't know what the shadow meant; I was old enough to see everything, hear everything, and yet understand nothing. The other eye was shut, sunken in its socket. Whenever I asked if I could touch the crumpled eyelid, he let me. He would crouch down in front of me, gathering his sarong between his dark, shiny legs, and I would run my finger lightly over the depressed surface between his eyebrow and his cheekbone. The skin there was delicate, extremely soft, and each time I was astonished. I knew how stiff fallen birds became. I still remember our dog's frozen mouth, all his teeth bared in a threatening grimace. With Roy, I learned that something dead could also be delicate and soft.

Every time Rada stepped down from the tuk-tuk, she said something to Roy, taking his hands in hers, words that delighted him and made him nod repeatedly. Then she went into the house, gave my parents a warm greeting with a kiss on the cheek. They had known each other for ages: Rada and my mother were born in the same village and had had the same classical dance teacher; until they were sixteen, they had performed as a duo in every corner of the country; they had met my father in university where he had started a drama club. My mother's interest in dance waned in favour of my father, so Rada began dancing solo and set up her dance school, which she regularly took abroad. I heard these facts in dribs and drabs; they circled around me, flitting in and out like moths. I didn't know how to tame them, how to stop them so I could connect them. What I cared about was seeing these three grown-ups together for a few minutes before my class, seeing them act as if I didn't exist yet or didn't exist anymore. My mother and Rada were so close that their heads touched, they let out snorts of laughter. Rada sometimes patted my father's shoulder. They got serious, solemn, whispered, shook their heads, then they were happy again. They switched between all their languages, often in the same sentence and, to my ears, it was like the sound of rain running through the waterspout: sharp, bright, smooth. At last Rada turned to me and, with that, a life of whirling began.

She put on a Bharatanatyam sari, took out wood sticks and little bells and, on the west side of the veranda, we started class with some yoga to warm up and stretch our muscles. That was followed by the adavus, the different leg, foot, arm, hand and neck poses. *Tat tai taam dith tai taam*. That was the hardest, most demanding part because Rada was exacting. *The adavus are the letters of the alphabet*, she would insist, *how can you read if you haven't learned them all, how can you be a Bharatanatyam dancer if you haven't mastered the adavus? How will you ever go onstage?* She pressed on my shoulders so my knees would stay bent, she lifted my elbows when they slumped, and with a finger she tapped my chin so I would raise it, so that my neck would be stretched, my bearing regal. With her voice intoning the syllables, with the wood sticks striking a rhythm, I followed her commands and moved from one pose to the next. Sometimes we wrapped up as the sky over the rice field was already turning red. Sometimes she decided that I had done a good job. Then she would rim my eyes with kohl, pin a sun-shaped ornament in my hair, tie the bells to my ankles, and I could perform the first of the Bharatanatyam dances, the Alarippu, the flowering bud. My parents appeared, almost shy; Aya emerged from the kitchen; and I knew that Roy was somewhere in the garden, watching me as well with the eye that wasn't dead. Then I danced to honour the god of dance, to honour my teacher. I danced as if sharing this stage with the setting sun and the beauty of all dancers past and future. I danced and, like the folds of my sari, like my body, my mind was set free and whirling.

Twice a year, Rada held a Bharatanatyam recital at the village temple. She brought several girls from the capital, each one prettier than the last, and everyone in the village came, even those who never went to temple, even Roy, even my father. There were the girls who played gods and their consorts, and there were the other dancers, often cast as village girls, dressed in more modest saris, simple ornaments, their ankles adorned with a single strand of bells. They had less training, they struck the same poses over and over, but they furnished the backdrop against which the two main characters could shine. When I was ten, Rada gave me the role of one of those main girls. I might have been short and slim and flat-chested enough to look like a little boy, but I thought of myself as a celestial nymph, danced like I was an apsara. At twelve, I was one of the consorts: my sari was gold and red, I wore four anklets with bells and I had on stage make-up. When I moved especially fast, my long plait whipped around my waist. Every face tilted up to me, admiring, besotted, as if looking at the gods. How could anyone believe that such moments of grace would not last? How could a girl be expected not to dream of whirling in a golden sari forever, as at her feet lay flowers flowers flowers?

It was a life unlike any other, with secrets, contradictions and ghosts: my mother could read cards, stars, palms and sometimes faces. On the last two days of the ascending moon, she became another woman who kept me at arm's length, let down her hair, walked through the garden at night, and no longer slept in her bed. I had no idea how such things happened, how they were known and whispered, but, during this time, people came to see her. They arrived on foot, walking hurriedly along the rice field, bent over, as if afraid of being noticed. Sometimes I listened at doors. Those people asked her to read their future, their children's, their partners'. They asked her what should be done so that two people who no longer loved each other could love each other again. They asked her how to mend broken ties between parents and children, how to make sure that nothing would ever go to pieces. They asked her to tell them how compatible two people would be in a prospective arranged marriage. They wanted to know if hearts were pure or crooked, if the dead were benevolent or malicious. They addressed my mother with the respect reserved for sages and rulers. When they went, they left behind fruits, homemade cakes, sweets, fabrics, saris, leather sandals, never money. Money thwarted readings, money thwarted my mother. There were also people who came during those stretches but didn't ask to see my mother. They, too, were silent, almost invisible. They sprinkled red powder in front of the gate at nightfall, slit cocks' throats, burned large candles before clay dolls. Our dogs scared them off, but then our dogs died because they licked the red powder. For those few days, my father kept me in school for many more hours. Aya was silent, surly, and slept on a mattress in my bedroom, by the door. Roy followed me when I played in the garden. I wasn't allowed to go near the rice field or to go with Aya into the village. Rada didn't come. Those adults put up a barrier between my mother and me, between the truth and me. I was told, in hushed tones, *Don't go up to your mother, don't talk to your mother, don't look your mother in the eye, let her walk barefoot on the gravel, no that's not your mother yelling, that's an animal in the wood, no she's not shouting your name, you heard wrong, no she isn't singing in the dark, no she isn't crying, you must have been dreaming, no that isn't a cock with a slit throat in front of the gate, the dog died because he was sick, we'll get another one.* It was very odd for me because I did see, I did hear, and sometimes I did know. It was as if through the barrier my father, Aya and Roy had put up, I glimpsed that woman who was my mother, I caught sight of the truth of our reclusive existence, but there was no touching or reaching any of that. When it was over, my mother became once more the woman who loved me from dawn to dusk, who suddenly pulled me into her arms to cover my face and neck with loud kisses, who said, *Yes, Vivi*, when I begged for something. Out of fear, or maybe cowardice, I kept holding off on asking her what she was.

In their bedrooms, Aya and Roy each had an altar with a black, gleaming stone idol. They made offerings of flowers, burned incense, and sometimes they would be tired after having fasted out of respect for this idol. On New Year's Day, Aya and Roy each hung up a garland of mango leaves on their bedroom doors. They told me it brought luck and warded off the evil eye. I made one for my bedroom but my father forbade me from hanging it. The sap was pungent and sticky on my fingers. *In this house we only believe in facts and science*, my father told me. But I myself would have liked to make some space in my heart for a stone statue, I would have liked to experience this devotion that went so far as starvation, I would have liked to believe in the power of mango leaves.

My father went on the radio and said things that scared my mother, Aya and Roy. In the evenings, I heard my mother pleading: *Why won't you keep quiet? Why do you have to provoke them? You promised me you wouldn't play politics! You have to think about us! We need to get out of here!* One day, after my father had spoken on the radio, Roy disappeared. I caught my mother and Aya talking in the language I wasn't supposed to use in the house. They looked at me as if I had no business there. I asked where Roy was, and my mother grabbed me by the arm. *There's no Roy anymore! He's had enough!* After that, for several days, I sat on the front steps, my fingers forming a telescope, and I waited for Roy to come back.

When we went into the village, my father didn't let go of my hand. All eyes followed us, the rich atheists from the huge house, the girl who danced but didn't go to school, the man who went on the radio and even TV to say that all this country's inhabitants were the same, that every soul should have the freedom to pray to the god he wanted to or not to believe in just one god, that the leaders were idiots, the man who spoke several languages in the same sentence, the husband of the sorceress. Those glares became a swell behind our back. As the years went by and the swell grew, I had the feeling that it was hissing at us, berating us. At those moments I couldn't get back to the house soon enough to find my mother, Aya, the school in the alcove, the evenings listening to music and playing cards. I started wishing I wouldn't grow up, wouldn't understand, would stay as I was: Vijaya in the grown-ups' shadow.

For a long time, I was convinced that this was how life was, chopped up into mouthfuls, cut up into morsels. Bougainvillea and hibiscus, water iris, my voice echoing in the well, frangipani flowers, my parents' laughter, the moon bewitching my mother, banana trees and palm trees, frogs croaking and birds chirping, ants in single file, endless homework and lessons, Aya's thin pancakes which I gulped down while they were still piping hot, coconuts thudding on the ground, the beehive behind the house, the dark clouds that always massed above

the wood and the rain I awaited because I liked to hear the
first drops on the roof, my father's unwavering voice on the
radio, Rada's wood sticks, *tat tai taam dith tai taam*. For a
long time I was sure everyone around me, everyone I loved,
was eternal.

But in the middle of a day not long before the rice harvest,
when the reeds were at their tallest, three days after my father
went on TV and opened his mouth, while I was learning how
to break down and solve the maths problem $2(x + 6) = 70.8$,
Aya started shouting. It was a mix of words in her language
and sharp cries. I had no idea whether those words meant fear
or insult, resistance or goodbye. I wish I'd remembered them
so I could repeat what she said before she died. In a single
stride, my father reached the window and I, too, unthinkingly
got up from my desk. A pickup truck was in front of the gate
and four men in khaki pants and sleeveless T-shirts, with
four white horizontal lines streaked across their brows, tried
to break the padlock on the gate with what I thought at first
were sticks. Aya, in the courtyard, was waving her arms and
shrieking. Suddenly there was a sound like a crack and she
bent over. I thought she was looking for a stone to throw at
those men, like she often did with wandering dogs, but she
kept bending over until she was flat on the ground. My father
clapped his hand over my mouth. Did I scream the moment
I realised what the sticks and the crack actually were? I don't
remember. He grabbed me by the arm, dragged me to the big
safe by the door where he kept his papers. He brought a finger
to his lips and our eyes met. His were the colour of the earth
after rain. He smiled at me for one second, perhaps, but in

that second was my whole existence. With his free hand he opened the hulking mass and an instant later I was inside.

Deafening was this pounding heart. Deafening was the blood rushing to my brain. I opened and shut my mouth, unsure what words to utter, what shrieks to let out, what prayers to think up. I heard nothing, I saw nothing, but in the safe's darkness, I felt the reverberations of what the four men were doing. For every blow, every attack, every torture, my huddled-up body, far, far away from those of my parents, absorbed the shock of what was happening in this huge house where my life had been one of deliciousness, warmth, whirling, a life unlike any other.

6

Nobody ever explained to me what it means to be a girl in this country. Nobody told me: be careful how you run through the rice field while flapping your arms like you want to fly, don't sing like that every morning when you wake up, be careful smiling at just anyone, don't lie down on the veranda next to the dog to listen at the door when people come to see your mother, don't sit in your father's lap every night, don't wash your hair by the well if someone can see you, don't steal the black seed oil out of your mother's cabinet to rub into your hair, don't be rude and laugh when you win at belote, don't start dancing when your favourite song about love and grief comes on the radio, and above all, don't ever, ever pick up a freshly fallen frangipani flower to tuck behind your ear.

Nobody told me that on the road, beyond the garden, the row of banana trees, beyond the rice field, there are people who watch how the girls grow up, who notice their busts swelling under their blouses, their heights increasing, their hips widening. Nobody told me that I was stupid when I claimed that someday, for real, I would grow wings and fly, free as a bird. Nobody told me that now I had to dance with less desire, less passion, that it would be best to remove my bells, my lipstick, my kohl, and that, on the feast day after a fast, it would be wise to play the role of the village girl rather than one of the consorts whose lips did not move even as her body danced all the languages of love.

Nobody ever told me: listen carefully to the radio when they talk about people taken from their beds by soldiers in the middle of the night and when they say the death was brutal, the death was violent. Nobody told me: ask your father what death by necklacing means; ask your mother what a ruined girl is; ask that cook you fondly call Aya where her family is, how she chose among her three children when the army asked her for one to prove her loyalty; ask Roy how his eye became dead, find out why he left. Nobody told me: listen carefully to the radio, one day you'll be the one kneeling. Nobody told me: enjoy the sky, the earth, the water while you still have the time. Savour it, dig in, swallow it, gorge on what you can; soon it'll be gone. Soon you'll know what it means to be a girl in this country.

7

I was in a place where I could see the beaten-earth courtyard and the old neem tree planted right in its centre. The foot of the tree was ringed by flat stones that children sometimes came to sit on. Our neem was especially big and tall and healthy and leafy, and Aya made good use of its leaves and seeds. I looked at the tree and tried to remember: crushed leaves to treat headlice, the liquid from steeping them for worms in the gut, a tisane made from them for stomach problems, the seeds' oil to soothe sore muscles, powdered bark to deter rodents. I dug deep into my memory to grab some moving image for each use, so that every one would be like a little film of its own, full of the garden's light, my parents' voice, Aya's hands. I could sit and watch the neem tree for ages, slowly replaying the scenes in my head, and that way maybe I could fall into a trance like those ascetics I'd seen in documentaries about breaking free of time and illusions. That way, hopefully, my physical body could stay here while my mind would be free to return to our house, to go to the capital to find Rada, to turn back time, or so on; this life, this body, this reality wouldn't matter anymore.

I was in a place where I could see Roy and some other men sitting in a half-circle on red plastic chairs under the corrugated metal awning. They were drinking beer, smoking cigarettes, but I couldn't hear what they were saying. People whispered here; even the children played at low volume. There wasn't any music or TV or radio. Night fell and under the lightbulb's weak gleam, they became indistinct, their contours and colours blurred into those of the chairs, the wall, the earth. At one point, Roy got up, stood in the centre of the half-circle. He was in a sarong and a light shirt, and he started gesturing. My parents and I had played that game where we had to use our hands to get people to guess a film or song or book. For a second, I thought he was doing that with his friends. Then he lay down on one side, in a foetal position, and pulled his knees into his chest, forming a ball. He shook his head hard, stretched his arms out, and dug them under his legs, as if fighting against someone who wanted to pull him upright. I couldn't make out his friends' faces. Were they fascinated by Roy? Were they laughing? Were they about to figure out what film or song or book it was? After a minute, he got up. Then lay down flat, got halfway back up, moved forwards on his knees, crawled, stood up. His body was double-jointed, a puppet, but with every step he seemed to become more coordinated. His limbs now stood him practically upright. He was moving forwards faster and then started running like mad around the neem tree while waving his arms. An icy chill seized my belly silently, ran through my chest, froze my heart. I had a good idea of what Roy was pantomiming.

He returned to his chair. Before picking up the beer he'd set on the ground, he turned in my direction. I jerked back from the window even though I was in the dark and he couldn't possibly see me. I dropped to the floor, curled up, my head between my knees.

I was in the safe again.

I stayed put, my arms locked around my folded legs, clinging to my father's smile, and I waited. Ridiculous thoughts stopped seeming so ridiculous: it was a prank; it was a dream; it was a historical re-enactment my father had set up to test my knowledge. The safe would open to show my parents and Aya bent over laughing at this joke they'd shared at my expense; I'd wake up in my bed and the pop music my mother loved would reach my ears. This was what people did during the war, they curled up inside furniture, they didn't make any sound, they didn't panic even if they were shaking in terror, even if they were peeing themselves, even if they were only thirteen: they just waited to be found.

Time has the consistency of rubber when you're afraid, it's like a Dali painting, it melts, it warps, it drips and there's no way to know whether it's day or night, if only a few minutes have gone by or hours on end.

When the safe opened and I felt a hand on my shoulder, I clutched my legs even more tightly, trying to curl up on myself like a louse. The hand was insistent, strong, it pried loose one arm, then the other, but I yanked them back, locked them under my knees, it shook me harder and harder and, as if it were at the far end of a tunnel, I heard the voice that accompanied this hand saying my name. *Vijaya. Get up, Vijaya.*

Then, at last, when the voice said my nickname right by my ear, and I smelled standing water, I raised my head. *Vivi, Vivi*, Roy repeated, crying from his one eye, and I was reminded of how odd it was to see his face wet on only one side. He helped me out of the safe, I felt like my body had been broken into a messy heap of parts, I was stumbling, I fell, I got back up, I crawled, I opened my mouth but no words came. I was at the door, I was in the hallway, I was clutching the wall, the furniture. It was pitch-black night and, behind me, Roy held a torch shakily, he was crying, he kept saying my nickname, he was telling me to stop moving.

It was like a nightmare in which I was running with leaden legs, trying to yell in vain. There was something I wanted to get to, but I didn't know what yet. I didn't look in my parents' bedroom or in the living room, I didn't think to go into my bedroom. Something else was calling me, an echo, a ghost. I got to the veranda and, with Roy's help, I pulled myself up, leaned against the railing. I would have given anything for some respite so I could take in the moonless night one last time, behold those thickets of stars, but there was no escaping the brutal smell and the sight of the still-red pyre in the lane leading to the house.

I hurtled down the steps and started running around the pyre in which I couldn't tell who was who now, where skin ended and rubber tyre began, who was still glowing red, if this was my mother's hand, if that was my father's shirt, where that bitter smell was coming from, if that was Aya's sari, if that was the blood of all three of them, I was running.

My father taught me that, in Hinduism, newlyweds go

around a fire seven times. There I was, going around that pyre, unable to stop myself, as if wedding my own misfortune, as if marrying the horrific end of my childhood, as if I wanted to yoke myself to life, to death, to this inhumanity.

In the night, Roy came into the room where I was sleeping alongside three other children. They didn't talk to me. They got up in the morning, pulled on school uniforms, and only came back to sleep. They had moved their mattress as far away as possible from mine. They clung together, and they never let go of each other's hands, not even in their sleep. Sometimes they played in the courtyard. They talked to Roy and the woman who was there, but I didn't understand at first who exactly they were. Even though he didn't work near ponds and rice fields anymore, Roy still smelled like standing water, and my nose alerted me well before his footsteps reached my mattress. He crouched down by me, set his hand on my eyes in hopes that I would close them, that I would fall asleep. He asked me how I was, if I needed something. Sometimes he brought his face to my hand and asked me if I wanted to touch his eye the way I did before, but I didn't talk, I didn't move, I didn't look.

He whispered nonsensical words but who was I to say what was sensical and what wasn't? He spoke of a place by the water, of his father who fished on stilts, he said he liked water but not the sea which scared him, he talked about his dead eye which saw things at nightfall and that was how he had an inkling about me, he sang old songs in languages I didn't know but which my father had sometimes used. His voice was hoarse, his throat coated with a bile that he hawked up and swallowed back down. He told me about what he'd eaten at midday or yesterday or last week, he described the monkey in the tree that watched him while he was washing himself. I didn't move, I listened. Maybe I knew that some other story would come in due time, one that would make me get up.

I didn't count how many nights went by that came with the smell of standing water before he told me about my parents.

Roy said:

Your father wasn't afraid of anything. He believed that his education and his friends would protect him.

He recalled:

Your mother had powers, but people didn't like that. They were afraid. She knew bad things were coming. She warned your father but he didn't believe in those sorts of things. He said, *I believe in science, in facts!*

Roy whispered:

I warned him, though, I'd heard people talking, I told him to keep quiet, I told him what had happened to other men before him, but your father was stubborn! Your father had studied abroad and he thought things that aren't thought here. He married your mother who was of a different religion. I don't have any religion, that was what he said on the radio, I don't have any language, all languages are mine, all religions are mine. How can anyone say something like that? If I hadn't been there, what would have become of you? If they'd found you, do you know what they'd have done to you? That father of yours was a proud man, far too proud, far too sure of himself.

Roy hissed:

Your father should have kept that mouth of his shut.

I sat up suddenly and spat in his face. Roy fell back, on his bottom, stifled a cry of surprise. The children shifted in their sleep but did not wake up.

You're the one who should keep that mouth of yours shut.

I didn't recognise my voice, hoarse, steely, like those marketplace women who badgered customers all day long. It wasn't the voice of some *kutti* anymore, it wasn't the voice of Vivi anymore.

After that, there were days when I got up. The lady who lived there was Roy's cousin, her name was Mani. The three children were hers. They had names but I never could remember them; the time when I'd dreamed of brothers and sisters, when I had imaginary friends, was long past. Whenever Roy showed up, I didn't let him out of my sight. I wanted to go back home, I wanted to know what he was doing at our house that night, why he'd disappeared without saying goodbye, I wanted to understand how he'd known that I was in the safe, I wanted to know everything. I might have been short, I might have been a girl, but I caught this grown-up man by the scruff of his neck, I grabbed his hand and clenched it until I could feel his bones. I wanted to poke out his other eye. Roy didn't say anything, he just shook his head. When I yelled, Mani gathered all her children in the bedroom. When the smell of standing water got so strong I was nauseous, I jumped on him, I wanted to know why he'd taken me out of the safe, what right he'd had to do that, who'd let him into our house. I hit him as hard as

I could, he just blocked the punches. I asked him if he was the one who'd killed my parents, and at that a thick tear came from his dead eye but I didn't care. I bit into the arm he was using to protect himself, and his skin was like a ripe mango that gave way under my teeth but his taste was far from sweet, it was metallic and those days that was what I needed.

On days like that, Roy and Mani shut me in the metal shed behind the house. There was an iron bedframe there, a straw mattress that was like lying on hundreds of red ants. It smelled like metal, it smelled like droppings. The lightbulb dangling from the ceiling crackled. In the shed, when I'd finished screaming, hitting, biting, I went limp. My body got stiff, I didn't feel the prickly straw or the harsh ground, I didn't think about my parents anymore, I wasn't scared anymore, I wasn't angry anymore, I didn't have memories anymore, where my heart had been I now had a hole.

For a long time, I went from the bedroom to the shed, from the shed to the bedroom. I could be calm for days. I would get up, I would shower, I would put on the dresses that Mani gave me, I would scrub the courtyard with a broom and its *swish swish* would soothe me, I wouldn't talk, I would look at the neem tree, the present would give way to my memories. There was no television here, no newspaper, no radio. When Mani went out, she locked me in the bedroom and I curled up in a ball in a corner and the room became another safe. One night the moon was so big that it seemed like it was trying to break free of the sky. That night, I yelled for my mother at the top of my voice and the dogs started barking. One day, I heard a prayer procession pass behind the wall surrounding the house and, at the sound of brass instruments, I started doing my adavus. They weren't perfect so I practised and practised until Mani dumped a bucket of water on my head. I thought that maybe I should trust the cycles of the moon to count the days going by, but why would I want to measure the time separating me from those I love?

And yet this respite was short-lived: all of a sudden I was suffocating from Roy's odour, from how one of those kids laughed, from the reddening embers in Mani's kitchen. Inevitably, some sound, some smell, some image would come and reawaken the mean dog. That was what the children called me, "mean dog", and when their words found me on all fours, locked in the shed, yelling who knows what, they weren't wrong.

8

The first time, he didn't look at me even though I was right there, sitting in the kitchen. Mani had asked me to chop the okra, she'd shown me how to do it, saying it was easy, and careful I didn't cut myself, and yet I couldn't help slicing them thin the way I'd seen Aya do it. I'd hold the okra in my left palm and run the knife under the skin to remove a layer that wasn't too thick or too thin. The knife was dull: I knew Mani had given me that one on purpose, she was scared of what I might do with a sharp blade. I sliced the vegetable carefully, long layer by long layer, with my back and head bent. A translucent sap dripped, turning my fingers sticky. Mani sighed. In the time I'd been staying with her, there had been things like this she didn't argue about. Maybe she recognised the shadow that fell over my face when, in my mind, I returned home, maybe she saw that letting me focus this way on a task, and one task only, let the mean dog sleep longer.

He didn't knock, he let out a hello in the doorway. Mani exclaimed, *Oh, it's you!* She clapped her hands together and walked out of the kitchen. She invited him to stay, sit down, have a cup of tea, but he told her he didn't have much time today. Deep within this daydream where I was in our kitchen with Aya teaching me how to slice okra lengthwise, where I was the mischievous but good little girl, where I was still her *kutti*, where I was once more my parents' Vivi, in this fantasy where the safe and the pyre didn't exist, his deep, soft voice found me. He didn't talk fast while swallowing his words the way Roy, Mani, their friends, the children did. I left Aya, I looked up, I saw his profile, he was looking at Mani, he was smiling. He said that his family had arrived this morning for their holiday and that they'd sent him over to find out if Roy might be willing to have a look at the garden. I was fascinated by his way of talking, I wanted to get up close to him, open his mouth, and see how the words bounced around and became rounded in there. He asked Mani how things were going and she suddenly lowered her voice, forcing him to lean in to hear her. I guessed she was telling him about me but he didn't look up at me the way most men would when told about a mean dog, a crazy girl, a survivor, a caged animal. He stood up, simply nodded, then left. *Come back for tea*, Mani called out after him as he headed off.

When Mani came back into the kitchen, I asked her, *Who was that?* and she startled. She narrowed her eyes at me and it took me a few seconds before I realised it was the first time I'd ever spoken to her. She reached out to my face but stopped herself before touching it, maybe I'd flinched, maybe she'd seen a shadow flicker over it. She took a deep breath. She sat down in front of me and started talking to me hurriedly, *Areyoualright, Didyoudecidetotalk, Roywillbesohappytoknow-*

that . . . I could see she wasn't going to answer my question so I bent my back and my head and I returned to my okra. Mani talked for a bit longer, cajoling me, but I wasn't listening anymore. I was still there, though, a big warm hand rested on my chest, I recalled the round, clear voice, I thought about how he didn't look at me. I was convinced, even though I had no way of being sure, that he'd gone to the trouble of leaving me a few shreds of dignity. And so I called him the boy.

The boy came back every so often, sometimes he stayed for tea, sometimes he played with the children, sometimes he just stopped by. Wherever I was, he looked around for me and gave me a nod. When I could, I watched him: he wore khakis and cotton shirts like one of those grown-ups who worked in the city, but he was as limber as a child and he threw his head back whenever he laughed. He had patent leather shoes, like the ones my father had worn when headed to the capital. I'd come to realise that he was a boy who lived in the capital and spent his holidays in this village where his grandparents had a house with a garden. Did that garden, too, have a well and a pond that Roy cleaned regularly? Maybe I could ask him to take me back with him, maybe he knew Rada and her dance school. But I didn't talk. In his eyes, I was a girl who often lay down flat, who was sometimes shut away in the shed at the back of the courtyard, maybe Mani had told him that I was a simpleton. I just watched him, he was both familiar and new. He reminded me of something that wasn't painful, that was connected to my past life but not to my unhappiness. Maybe he was like an old dream that had never come true or a hope that I'd clung to.

The first time he approached me, Mani and Roy weren't there. The children were in the courtyard, they'd drawn hopscotch squares. I knew they were watching me. I could tell from the way they were playing in silence, with measured movements, looking out of the corners of their eyes at me sitting on the ground under the awning. When the boy came, they went crazy, they swarmed him, they were all talking at the same time, trying to climb up his back, they'd forgotten about me. He told them something or other to calm them down, then pulled things out of his pocket, probably sweets. He stayed under the neem tree for a minute, watching the children gobble them down and then go back to playing hopscotch. Then, to my great surprise, he headed over to me, walking as if his feet barely touched the ground, was he perhaps a dancer? He sat down beside me. There was no time for me to pull away as his arm brushed mine. He said, *Pardon me*, and shifted back a few centimetres. I wondered if the distance meant he would notice the front of my dress fluttering because my heart was starting to pound in my chest, I wondered if he could smell me, there was no more black seed oil to rub into my hair, there was no more rose perfume to dab behind my ears, there was no more olive oil soap to soften my knees and elbows. I wondered if I smelled like an orphan now, like a mean dog, like the safe and the pyre. Maybe, at this point, I smelled like the mattress I slept on, humid, sweaty, rancid – how could I possibly know?

The boy stayed on the ground and did not move, he breathed and my presence did not bother him, he didn't feel obligated to speak to me. The children played, they were singing a nursery rhyme as they hopped, the sky's patterns shifted through the neem tree's foliage, the wind rose then fell. I no longer felt like I had a live wire running down my spine, I relaxed, maybe I even sighed. I was here, I was real. It occurred to me that the children had grown, they had been so small the first time I'd seen them. After a long stretch free of waiting and fear, he brought his fist up to my face, then turned it over. His fingers with pale nails were holding something. He waited for me to make a move, maybe this was a game where I had to guess what was in his hand, maybe I had to blow on it for it to open, maybe I had to say some magic word or press my lips to it, how was I to know what this boy wanted from me? It had been so long since I'd played anything. When he opened his fingers, his palm was a plain with brown furrows, on which rested two pale, silvery insects. I knew that couldn't be right but that was what I imagined, that was what I wanted to see. When he shook his hand lightly, the pale, silvery insects touched and their wings rustled. Maybe they were butterflies. They were very beautiful and I didn't move out of fear that they might fly off. He closed his fingers over them and drew his fist back as slowly as he'd presented it to me. Time stopped.

The boy believed he was opening a sweet, but it was clearly a bug he was peeling and bringing to my lips. I opened my mouth. He thought he was offering me something smooth and inert and minty but it was a ribbed, beating, sweet heart that he gave me. I caught his fingers gently between my teeth and began licking and sucking them. He let out a small, unguarded cry. I wanted to swallow his whole hand with its brown ruts that told his fate, those lines that my mother could have deciphered when the moon was high in the sky, I wanted to swallow all the gleaming insects and all the wings' rustling. Where did this liquid warmth filling my belly, running down to my thighs, come from? What was this feeling with no thorns attached to it, this feeling I had never felt before? I was falling gently into an unknown, delicious void emanating from the boy, it was making me forget who I was, where I was, where I'd come from. His own shirt was fluttering now, the distance was gone, his breath sped up while I licked and sucked, while I nibbled and wetted. I clutched his wrist, the truth was I wanted to swallow him whole and forget what had been.

I felt a sharp pain on my forehead and the boy yanked back his hand. He got up and ran over to one of Mani's children who was about to throw another stone. A warm liquid collected in my eyes and before I passed out I heard the children shout, *Mean dog!*

9

I didn't ask him his name when he came back. I didn't ask him where he'd been, what he'd done during those hours I hadn't kept track of, given that here in the shed there was no day or night. I woke up with a thick bandage around my head. The shooting pain where the stone had hit me felt like it was following this strip of fabric, tracing circles upon circles. Radiating in rings upon rings.

Mani brought me food and drink. She led me to the bathroom. She changed the cloth and undressed me to scrub my body with a coarse rag. She slipped one of her dresses patterned with lots of small red and white and blue flowers on me. She pressed bitter pills and gluey brews to my lips. She wiped my mouth. When I bled for the first time and stained the mattress, she scoured my whole body with almost unbearably hot water. I was sure I was going to die, I thought the wound on my forehead had caused internal bleeding, I saw the huge poster in the alcove again, the one showing a human body and its innards, and I imagined my organs breaking down and pouring out of me. She folded a bit of fabric into a thick rectangle and placed it in my knickers.

I wasn't dead.

I watched her tend to this body which was mine but which, in her hands, had no brain. It had no heart or mind, it had no soul. Mani never talked to me, she never met my gaze, her hands never lingered or caressed. I could feel the anger she bit back and the desire she had not to see the living being in this body. If I resisted, if I started yelling or made her look at me, she left. Sometimes I wished she would treat me like a dog, that she, too, would throw a stone at my head, that she would curse me. I might have sobbed, spoken, said sorry, asked why, but she was unwavering, her attempts to erase me bordered on vicious. She did what she had to do, she made sure nothing in the shed was where it shouldn't be, she turned the lightbulb off and back on, *click click*, and she double-locked the door behind her. I stayed on my bed, filled with horrible fear, and I had no idea whether it resulted from the deep loneliness I'd been cast into by my parents' death, or from the feeling of not knowing what this body was anymore – mean dog, girl, woman, ghost? – or whether it was a reaction to Mani's attitude, or to this lightbulb's mere crackling.

So, when the boy came back, I didn't ask him his name, I didn't ask him how he'd found me, how he'd managed to get in here without Roy or Mani noticing. At first I reasoned it was a dream; I didn't move. I kept my back straight, my fear slowly giving way to a feeling I couldn't name, couldn't have guessed might exist in me. It began in my belly and gradually spread outwards, blooming in my heart and rushing between my legs. It fed on loss, loneliness and curiosity. It was a powerful, magical feeling that wiped away my thoughts. Maybe that was what kept me alive in this shed, maybe that feeling had kept me somewhat intact.

The boy approached me, his face brightened when he passed below the lightbulb's halo, shadows ran over his features, I didn't know what they meant or where they'd come from, but they didn't scare me. He sat down beside me and I could smell his cleanness, his clothes had been washed not long ago, his body had mingled with lemon soap, his hair was soft and fine like the tips of a thousand blades of wild grass swaying in the wind. He extended his hand to me and I realised how hungry I had been.

Maybe it was a dance that, like Bharatanatyam, could only properly be performed once all the adavus were mastered, but here I couldn't say who was the teacher and who the student, I couldn't say whether the day engendered new variations, the night new desires. He, too, licked my fingers but preferred my lips. For months I had had no voice but now I was discovering that, in his mouth, my tongue was keen to speak, to tell, to learn new languages.

Time flowed in kiss after kiss, embrace after embrace. Maybe it was a dance, a choreography from another time, another land, that required bodies to become waves that rose and fell, a ballet of backwash, a tidal tango.

In the days that followed, Mani scoured me with even more force, as if she wanted to scrub off the smell of lemon, the perfume of desire. As if I were resisting that erasure.

With the boy, I discovered that my body, once so small, so

knobbly, had changed. It could be grabbed by the handful now, squeezed, caressed, kneaded, swallowed down and drunk up. A body that inhaled and expelled, that pulled tight and set loose. Sometimes the thought occurred to me that this body could never fit back in the safe but when I thought such things the boy seemed to sense it in my tensing. So he rubbed my shoulders, he blew on my hands, he leaned in to lick my eyelids, he let me bury my head in his armpits, where the saltiness was strongest.

One evening, he handed me a newspaper clipping about the murder of a political opponent and his wife, and their daughter's disappearance. He held me close while I read the short article. I turned over the paper in hopes of finding a date but there wasn't one. The clipping was somewhat yellowed, soft. How many years had I been at Mani's? What was I supposed to do with what he'd given me, was he expecting me to talk to him about it, to tell him the name of this lost girl, to confirm his suspicions? I did none of those things, I gave him back the piece of paper, I gave him no answers, I just wanted to forget. He folded it up and slipped it back into his front shirt pocket, into which a pen had been tucked.

There wasn't anyone left to tell me what was true, what was imagined, what were lies and what were secrets. Where were the names of things, the origins of words, the inner workings of the universe? I forgot maths, biology, Latin, physics. I forgot the names of prime ministers and presidents, rivers and mountains, the ends of poems, the refrains of songs. There wasn't anyone to tell me how to grow up, I didn't know what was expected of me, I didn't know what awaited me.

Days went by and before me lay the sum total of what I didn't know about this world and sometimes I felt like my bed was a raft, that the ground was the bottomless sea of all those years remaining for me without anyone to tell me what to do, without anyone to hold my hand. When I cried out in terror, the children threw stones at the shed. Roy didn't come to crouch at the foot of my bed, Mani didn't come to clean me.

When I was alone, I sometimes found solace in nature. The vines winding between the sheet-metal sections, the grasses springing up in the corner of the door, splitting into three blades overnight, the shriek of birds at dusk, the flightless bugs leaving shaky lines on the ground, the humidity giving my skin a reptile's sheen, the electric smell of the air before a storm. It reminded me of the sensation I'd sometimes felt back home, of being on the edge of an untamed world that would never stop closing in around us, hemming in our homes and maybe engulfing us overnight. Could it be that I wasn't so far from the house after all? Could it be that if I managed to escape I might find the path through the little wood as I followed the birds' shrieks, as I inhaled the lush, loamy air around the rice field?

When he was there, the boy took me somewhere free of violence and safe and pyre and fear. I didn't know how to put words to what we were doing, love sex fever coupling heart food water being having our bodies spread flat like a map of the world for our fingers our mouths to explore, but while we were one and we were all these things my mind went quiet and I imagined gleams brightening here and there to light a path. While we were one and we were all these things I was

83

alive and not dwelling on returning home. All I wanted was to be here and now.

Sometimes I danced for him under the lightbulb's crackling. *Tat tai taam dith tai taam.* I was the god and his consort, I was both all the faithful and all those cast out, I was the forest and the desert, the flowering bud and the everlasting night. When I spun, there was no need for sari, bells, lipstick, kohl. My splendid nakedness was all the finery I could want.

10

They said I was a ruined girl. I didn't know what that meant.

Mani came each day to check my knickers. She squinted as she examined them, sniffed them, then she threw them in my face. How could I have known what she was looking for?

Mani and Roy dragged me out of the shed which I didn't want to leave now that I'd built a world of my own within its four sheet-metal walls, a world I knew the contours and limits of. I was intimately familiar with the lightbulb's crackle and the yellow puddle it cast on the ground, I had internalised the mattress's odour, the beaten-earth floor's texture, the geometric patterns that the sun traced and the scent that the night brought with its arrival. I was partial to the zigzagging of insects and the surprise of buds slipping between two sheet-metal panels. This was a geography entirely my own. This space was where the boy came to find me and, while it had been several nights since I'd last seen him, I still knew this space was where we had become what we were.

Mani and Roy were distraught, they had their heads in their hands, repeating that I was a ruined girl, they'd stopped

saying that I was a mean dog. Roy asked me if I'd thought
about my parents, he got close with his hand raised but he
didn't slap me. Mani, in turn, had found a long strip of wood
from somewhere and she stood in the doorway to give me a
hiding. The wood smacked my arms, my legs, but there was
something unreal about what she was doing, she was far
enough away from me that she had to take pains to keep the
plank horizontal, that the punishment was slow to reach me.

I understood that something terrible had happened
because of me, I understood that Mani and Roy couldn't sleep,
I listened to them talking for hours, unhappy, fighting, but at no
point did they actually tell me why they were angry with me.

I wondered what might have happened had Roy or Mani
not treated me like a being that had no mind, no will, no
desire, no brain. Had they not seen me as a dead weight they
couldn't shake off, had they been kind enough to simply talk to
me, to explain things the way my parents had a long time ago.

Roy left for some time and Mani made me sleep in her
bedroom with one of my ankles tied to the foot of her bed.
She wanted to keep me from going into the shed. She made
me drink bitter concoctions and swallow pills. I didn't know
what sickness she was trying to cure me of. I had diarrhoea,
I vomited, at times I felt like my belly would rip open, but I
obeyed her, I swallowed everything she gave me. Mani continued to check what was in my knickers and she wasn't happy.

But that was nothing compared to the grief that only grew
keener with each day I was apart from the boy. I didn't know
where he was. I wondered what I'd done to make him stop
coming. In the evenings, I stayed awake in hopes that he might

appear, I imagined him standing in the door, proffering his sly smile. I imagined him coming to untie me and take me to the shed. Sometimes I thought about him hard enough that I was sure I could see him sitting in the chair in the corner of the bedroom. He was leaning forwards, as if he wanted to tell me something. A pen stuck out of his shirt pocket, and the bulb's weak light sent shadows skittering over his face like a swarm of birds. I felt hot but still had goosebumps. When I saw him in this way and he looked at me so intensely it shook me, I said, *I love you*, I didn't know where those words came from, I don't know whether it was my mother or my father who had uttered them, I didn't know what song they harked back to, but I said to the boy as I imagined him sitting on the chair, *I love you, I love you, I love you.* I stepped into these words on my own terms, they were new on my tongue as if I were the first to dream them up and utter them.

The grief I felt here was different from the grief I'd endured with my parents. They coexisted side by side, the one the bottomless pain of what had been violently torn away, the other the disappearance of a future that had, just yesterday, been so tenderly offered to me. The two fed off one another and they kept growing.

One night, Roy came back and untied me hurriedly. Mani was there too; they led me to a car. They made me lie flat on the backseat and covered me with a plastic tarp. There was a man with very white hair driving and Roy sat next to him, his standing-water smell more oppressive than ever. Before the car door shut, Mani threw a bag at my feet. I sat up, I grabbed her arm and I said her name as tenderly as I could. I wanted to say thank you, to say goodbye, I wanted her to keep me near, I wanted to promise that I wouldn't be a mean dog or a ruined girl anymore, I wanted to show her my knickers, I wanted to know the boy's name. Somewhere between my parents' love, my childhood world, the dancing, the safe, the pyre, the shed and the boy's body, there was Mani. She was neither love nor affection nor body nor language nor home but she was a being I wanted to cling to. My voice screeched in the night of words beyond reach. Mani yanked her arm back and slammed the door shut. The car started and I looked back to see her running to the neem tree that I knew by heart from endless observation, her feet stamping the ground I'd swept so often. I prayed for her to turn back but, in her eyes and in her heart, I no longer existed.

On the backseat, I stretched flat, tucking the tarp's edges under me while leaving my head uncovered. I was full of tears but didn't let a single drop escape. I wanted to see the sky framed by the window and I wondered how my mother, that woman well-versed in the old language of heavenly bodies, would have read those stars. Would she have seen my destiny hanging in the balance or set in stone? Would she have insisted that I perform rites, that I fast, so I could be freed at last?

Huge raindrops pelted the car. I imagined a horde of children lined up along the road hurling gravel stones at the vehicle. The windows fogged up, the sky became a washed-out, shimmering fresco. Inside, the bitter odour of sweat mingled with that of standing water, and the breath the two men exhaled was that of a marsh teeming with countless little mouldering skeletons.

I couldn't remember how I'd first come to Roy's. One minute I'd been running around the pyre and the next I'd been looking at the neem tree in the courtyard. Had I, then as now, been lying in the backseat of a car, hidden under a tarp? Had I been sobbing and pleading for my parents or Aya? Had the presence of Roy and his dead eye reassured me?

This was a new route. It was a night with no stars, no moon, one of those interminable nights that threatened to stretch on and on and on.

This was a route I needed to commit to memory. I needed to take in every jolt, every instance of the car speeding up or braking, I needed to watch the treetops stark against the sky, now a forest, now a city with concrete structures and electrical wires strung between poles, now more trees spaced apart, now a wood, now the washed-out sky again. I needed to remember all of it, in order, and I had to be sure for a very long time that, if I wanted, I could follow this route in reverse. I had to be sure that I could, if asked, explain exactly how to get to me.

My skin had stretched, my organs had shifted to make space, my body had got bigger. There was no hiding me in a safe now. Did I still bear some trace of who I'd been, that Vijaya who was such a good student in the alcove, that Vivi who laughed with a mouth full of honey, that *kutti* who saw the world as her garden, that sated, naked dancer whirling for a boy? Did I need a new name for who I would be once I reached the end of this night?

11

There were times, the first year of our life together, when Emmanuel asked me what it had been like. *Tell me something*, he would whisper, and I knew what he wanted, I knew what he actually meant, that he actually wanted to say, *Give me something*, because, when we had sex, I'd always held back some part of myself, I'd kept it from flowing to him because I was afraid of what that part might hold, a flower, a fruit, a pomegranate, a stone, I didn't know whether that part I held tight between my legs knotted in my belly hidden in my heart buried in my throat, whether that part was nectar or poison.

I told him:

My bedroom walls were painted pink.

For breakfast there was yoghurt and honey.

One year, right after Christmas, there were little green short-tailed parrots flying every evening from palm tree to palm tree until the sun set.

I told him:

The sea was sometimes so pale and flat that you could

imagine getting all the way to the horizon and never slipping. I liked looking at it, I could have just climbed over the low wall and crossed the road, but I never did. There were poles stuck in the sand and, at high tide, fishermen would perch atop them and cast their rods.

I told him:

Every morning there was a man who cycled over with such a huge bundle of leafy branches, you couldn't see the bike's back wheels. He pedalled standing up, wearing a sarong.

Further away was a sculptor whose sweaty body was covered in wood dust.

Taut ropes had been strung between the huge palm trees and the tappers collecting sap walked up and down them.

Even further away were women in long dresses with patterns of small flowers who embroidered fabrics and laughed whenever a tourist stopped.

I told him:

At dusk, the flowers' perfume rose in the air like incense smoke.

Sometimes Emmanuel interrupted me. What was the colour of my bowl at breakfast, were the parrots perhaps dancing, was the yoghurt the extra-creamy kind or not, was the sculptor an old man or fresh-faced, what sorts of fish did the men on stilts catch, were the country's locals born acrobats if they were climbing poles and walking on ropes?

Because he was a good man, Emmanuel made do with these scraps to imagine what my life had been like before he'd met me. Because he was a man who thought he'd saved me from a country reduced to rubble and had done his part in helping to save the country itself, he didn't insist, he decided that he'd done more than his share. Because he was a man in love with me, he believed in the charm of what I told him, he never questioned the colours, the aromas, the images. And in seeing him as calm as a baby being told a wondrous tale, I too forgot that my words were lies, that the tenderness of this landscape I was sketching for him was a sham.

Because he was a man who had never truly experienced violence, he didn't know that, at times, I wished that he would try to hunt down this part of me that I held tight between my legs knotted in my belly hidden in my heart buried in my throat, that he would use a lance, a machete, his long fingers, that he would plunge into me to turn me inside out like a glove, that he would shine a light to examine my guts, my stomach, my crotch, my tongue, and in the end he would make me actually vomit spit expel climax speak.

I didn't let go of the bag that Mani had left for me. It wasn't heavy. Roy went ahead of me, walking quickly past the buildings gleaming in the early dawn. The car with the silent white-haired driver stayed at the gate. Upon reaching a long, narrow building, Roy knocked several times. *Amma! Amma!* I knew that meant "mother", but I knew that Amma was also the name used for a respected woman or an elderly lady on the street. That was what Roy called my mother and Rada. That was what Aya called my mother, who was thirty years younger than her: *kutti Amma*. Little mother. My heart, buoyed by wild hope, leaped in my chest. What if it was a familiar face that came to welcome us? What if this whole journey had been a return? I was stunned by this naïve heart; hadn't it learned anything? My mind, in contrast, knew there would be no divine intervention, no happy homecoming like in films, and forced my body to stay absolutely still. A woman in white opened the door and Roy gestured for me to stay outside. I held the bag close to my chest, pressing it against my heart to quieten it. They talked, their voices overlapped – Roy's was rushed, pleading; the woman's, calm and firm – but I didn't understand what they were saying, my ears were buzzing, my throat let out a sound like an empty pump. My thoughts weren't strong enough yet, they couldn't hold off the fear over-powering me in this unknown place, in the middle of what I understood to be abandoned temples.

It was the woman who came out first and she looked me up and down thoughtfully. Even in the half-light, I could tell she was weighing me up, judging me. She turned to Roy and nodded. He stepped back, brought his hands together, and slowly bent towards her several times, retreating, distancing himself. My body might have made a move to follow him, my mouth might have said something. The woman touched my arm, she did not exert any pressure, any force, but it was enough for me to understand. I was staying.

I watched Roy disappear. I might have thought of that moment with the pink lotus flowers that he'd strewn across my windowsill, I might have recalled how powder-soft his dead eye had been, and his tears when he opened the safe, I might have repeated in my mind the stories he'd come to whisper to me in the evenings. I might have been filling my

93

head with all these things so as not to remember how he broke into a run towards the car, away from me. Later on, at times when life was peaceful, I would convince myself that he had run because it would have broken his heart to say goodbye. At other times, however, I knew he was running the way a man runs from a house on fire.

In the office, as day broke, I realised that Amma was a very old woman. Long, fine wrinkles etched her face. Her features drooped down her face, as if they'd started to sag with the years. Brown spots dotted her hands. She didn't talk but pointed to where I should sit. She emptied Mani's bag: three dresses adorned with a floral pattern, some bread wrapped in a rag, and a pair of sandals. She looked each thing over carefully, sniffed at it, then put it back in the bag, which she shut. I got up to take it but she stopped me with a raised hand. I tried to grab the bag by reaching out to the table and she moved, gripping my hand. Her bony strength surprised me, but I didn't stop. That was my bag, those were my dresses, my bread, my sandals. We struggled for a few seconds, her hands tight around my wrists. Suddenly, she'd had enough. She slapped me so hard that I stumbled back. She walked up and slapped me again, several times, brisk harsh movements administered with her wrist, until I slumped into the chair. I could feel my face swelling, burning up. She pointed a finger at me and said, *Nothing belongs to you here.*

It was a lesson I would be taught again and again, in every way possible, until I felt like it was tattooed across my forehead.

In the courtyard children in white went by, their hair

cut short. Through the office windows, I saw them move briskly, single-file, heads bowed or looking straight ahead, some adjusted their clothes while walking but they made no sound and, soon, they disappeared. I wondered if I'd imagined that white flock but I didn't dare to get up and check. I didn't know that, soon enough, I would be part of this immaculate line and, from afar, I too would seem like a child. For the time being, that *Nothing belongs to you here* applied only to my bag and what it held. I didn't know yet that those words extended to the dress I was wearing, to my skin, my body, my thoughts, my sweat, my past, my present, my future, my dreams, to my very name.

The lesson began with being thoroughly sanitised in the showers at the centre of the building by the wood. A young woman was waiting for us. Amma said that I was to call her Akka, big sister, even though she couldn't have been much older than me. She was dressed in a long skirt that she'd hiked above her thighs. Her skin was dark, her legs swollen as if waterlogged. She was the one who would see to me. She had me undress and slathered my body with a thick, acrid paste. My hair, still in a long plait, was covered with some powder. When she got to my breasts, my bottom, and between my thighs, I recoiled but she held me in place, she patted me gently to keep me calm, she twisted my arm. Once I was caked from head to toe, once my eyes were stinging and I heard myself pleading, *Akka! Akka!* as if she were in fact my big sister, she sprayed me with water from a garden hose. She didn't speak to me and didn't look at me when she aimed the water at me and she asked me to spread my thighs, to raise my arms, to crouch down, to bend over. She looked at Amma who was standing in the doorway and who would order Akka to do it three more times. I must have looked truly filthy. My skin hurt from being scoured, my scalp stung, keeping my eyes open was painful, and my tongue was heavy with that bitter taste. I thought of the boy's hands exploring my body as if seeking out something that belonged to him and my legs slowly opening as if to welcome him home at long last, I thought of the dance I'd offered him with my body from before and now all these memories had been disinfected, scoured, scraped, rinsed. *Nothing belongs to you here.*

Akka gave me a sarong that I wrapped tight around myself. She pulled a chair onto the grey stone and I sat down. I was calm now, more or less dazed, I didn't argue when she placed a towel on my shoulders and grabbed my plait. I knew what was next, I finally understood exactly what Amma had said, her words swelled and gained meaning in the room's humid air. *Nothing belongs to you here.* Akka positioned the scissors at the base of the plait, she pressed the cold blades against my nape, and she cut, tugging with one hand and snipping with the other. Even for the sharpened metal, such thick hair was no easy matter, but the woman wielding the scissors was well practised; Akka in her big skirt, who said nothing, was well acquainted with the thick, curly hair of this country's girls, ruined and otherwise. After the plait gave way, the blades went on working for a good while all around my head, *snip snip snip*, until all that remained was a brown stubble along my skull. I knew that other girls had sat in this chair with this towel over their shoulders, their grief and their fear were still reverberating in this dank bathroom where the window high up was so grimy as to evoke a permanently low, grey sky.

I had enough time to spot my plait on the ground before it was wrapped up in a red cloth, like a long black snake crushed flat. I had a fleeting image of Rada on our terrace, beating the rhythm of my steps with her wood sticks, *tat tai taam dith tai taam*. I was hosed down again. I watched the locks of hair, like commas, whirling around before disappearing down a hole dug into the corner between the stone and the wall. *Nothing belongs to you here.* I understood what these women – the big sisters in skirts who were silent, the mothers who slapped – were doing, I understood how swiftly just one strand of hair could send me back into childhood, into my dreams of before where I imagined myself a dancer, flowers at my feet, ornaments in my hair, my long plait whirling around me.

They took me into another room where Akka, whose skirt was now lowered, poked my belly, my breasts. She pinched my nipples between her forefinger and her thumb. Then she mumbled something to Amma who had me swallow two pills and some sticky black stuff that made me want to throw up. But I swallowed the bitter bile in my throat, I pressed my lips together and kept my mouth shut the way my father hadn't.

They handed me undergarments, a shirt, a flared skirt. They were clean cotton clothes; their white was weathered grey here and there. I wasn't thinking about the pink and blue flower pattern on Mani's dresses anymore, my mind couldn't bear dwelling on that motif. They brought me a plate of rice and vegetables. I crouched down to eat and the

NATHACHA APPANAH

two women hovered over me, not talking, not making one unnecessary movement. I felt like they had found the bottom of my soul and knew what was in my chest. If only I could give them everything and not keep a thing for myself. I was so exhausted.

In a bed at the back of a dormitory with peeling walls on which some of the original pink paint could still be seen, I lay down. The two women watched me and muttered a name. I sat up to hear better. They repeated the name while looking at me, it wasn't mine but I was so sleepy, I was so exhausted. I wanted to correct them but Amma held up a finger and I curled up. The truth was that nothing belonged to me anymore, not here, not elsewhere, not ever. My name, my past, my memory were all erased. I slept as if falling down a dark well. At the bottom of this well was a thick carpet of hair, and I sank into it.

During this night or this lightless day, with my skin thoroughly scrubbed, my head relieved of its hair, my heart bereft of its name, my mind brought to heel, only one thing remained to be taken from me. These women who went by "Big Sister" and who wore long skirts, these others who went by "Mother" and whose faces had drooped with time, these women knew the bodies of ruined girls. They knew how to rip bellies open from the inside, how to tear out the bad vines that had attached themselves to inner walls and, as I began screaming, sobbing, they stayed on the banks of this nameless pain, they waited there for me to cross the waters with a body now wholly empty.

When I opened my eyes again, I couldn't say what time

it was, I couldn't say how much time had passed since Roy had left me there. If I had been told there and then that the outside world, not only this country but every continent, every island, every forest, every city, every freshwater bay and every rice field's border, if I had been told that the world, full of people with names and faces, had come to a stop, I would have believed it.

12

Like always, I was the first one awake and for a few seconds I felt as if something had yanked me out of my sleep: a dog barking, a bird shrieking, a voice calling. I sat up, I probed the darkness, I pricked up my ears, but, apart from a few girls snoring, there was nothing. I got up, I pulled a shawl over my shoulders, and I made my way out of the dormitory. It was easy: my bed was by the door. I crossed the hallway quickly and quietly, I went through the kitchen which never had its door locked.

I went around the building and ran all the way to the steps of the little temple in the courtyard. That was my favourite one. The one most desecrated by men, the one most ravaged by time, and now the one being slowly swallowed up by nature. Only a few paces away, the forest loomed. The structure was crumbling into the ground. It occurred to me that one morning I would wake up and it would be gone. Vines had covered the outer wall of the temple's back and burst into its sides. How could such a small stalk be strong enough to penetrate the slightest crack and split open concrete, stone, marble?

A long time ago, someone had told me that vines, not being trees, use what's around them to climb ever higher and get the most sun. This place, where vines crept across the ground like reptiles, felt like an exception. Could it be that in temples, or in the rubble of this temple, the best light was buried, hidden away? Maybe whoever had told me that didn't know the first thing about vines and was just spouting nonsense.

I sat on the steps for some time, I listened as the night-time noises – insects crawling, leaves rustling, branches snapping, wind howling – subsided. At high tide, even the waves' lapping was audible. Sometimes one of the dogs that roamed the grounds approached. It stayed at the foot of the steps and watched me with yellow eyes. It didn't bark, accustomed as it was to our odour of bleach, sweat and mould. I didn't like those dogs. They were both shy and wily; if shooed off with a few thrown stones, they would whine like puppies; if offered some bread from your hand, they would bite off your fingers; if the sun was high, they would stretch out, baring their pink, glistening genitals. The youngest girls were scared stiff of those dogs. Some were so thin that their backbones poked through their skin, making them look like prehistoric animals. I'd seen prehistoric animals before, in a book, a long time ago. If a dog looked like it was going to settle in, I drove it off with a snarl and a stamp of my foot. Maybe it, too, thought it was facing a prehistoric animal.

Within the darkness I felt no fear, as if it lay waiting to envelop me in its softness each night, a secret meeting I wouldn't miss for anything. It entered me just as much as I entered it. Sometimes I dreamed of being like the blackness of deepest night, at once visible and not. I stayed put, I tried not to think of yesterday or tomorrow or today. Just me and the depths of night. When the first sounds of day came – a rooster's crow, a metallic noise, a motor's growl – I entered the temple, I peed where there had once been an altar. I could see the sky, and what stars were still visible, through the gashed-open roof above me. When it rained, wherever I was, I was reminded of that spot, I told myself that the rain would wash away my pee and the thought made me smile.

If Amma could have seen me then, she would have gone into a rage and made sure there was hell to pay. She would have said I was no different from those who wreaked havoc on this place years earlier when people didn't pray to these divinities but turned to other gods in other temples. How could I explain to her that this was the only way I'd found to lay claim to something here? If I'd torn down the vines, washed the walls, cleaned the frescoes, if I'd burned incense each morning and set flowers down there, this place would have become beautiful in the eyes of all again and then it would surely have slipped out of my hands because everything that is beautiful is taken away. When I was so tired that my legs trembled, when I felt like the day would never end, when the yoghurt in the morning was so curdled that I couldn't keep it down, when the dusk in the dormitory stirred up tears and terrible stories, I took comfort in thinking of this place in rubble that awaited me, and me alone.

A portion of an orange fresco remained in the left corner of the back wall, depicting a procession of plump women with plaits down to their hips. They followed a chariot but hammer blows had effaced the figure perched on the conveyance. And the altar had been wrecked in turn by something stronger, in my head it was a cannonball, or a bomb, or a few hundred determined soldiers. Little was left apart from a cracked flagstone. I didn't try to imagine the idol that had been sculpted here, seated or lying flat, dressed in a plain saffron dress or a gold tunic. I didn't believe in gods, I didn't believe that they forgave hearts or answered prayers, but I knew that this place granted me something, what exactly I wasn't sure: a touch of courage, a surge of strength, a shred of night, a breath of hope.

A long time ago, someone had told me that gods and temples were invented by people who didn't believe in science, but what did he know, that man who opened his mouth and ignored those telling him he was putting his family in danger? Maybe those places where men and women came to worship imaginary beings were offering what science could not – something intangible, something ineffable that enabled them to face the day to come? Maybe the rites in those places warded off pyres and safes?

A century ago, this place had been a complex with seven temples of various sizes and some people had travelled all day and all night to prostrate themselves before various divinities here. The temples were strikingly white with gold trim. On the walls were frescoes depicting the tales that glorified the divinities and on the marble columns were sculpted women with voluptuous bodies. Each year, for the new year, the monks who had made lifelong vows to these gods washed the seven temples from top to bottom with scented water and hung garlands of gilded cloth between the structures. All around were flowers, incense, hordes come to pray and offer gold coins, money, jewels. I learned all this from Amma. Sometimes she felt compelled to tell me things; whether to reward me for a good day's work or just to hear herself talk, I couldn't be sure. She said, *Come over here*, and together we looked at black-and-white photographs that showed this temple complex at the height of its splendour. At those moments, her voice softened. I liked the close-up photographs – the frescoes, the sculptures, the friezes, the recesses for floor lamps, a woman's face. At times, Amma lingered on the one that showed a huge crowd praying in front of the main temple. I wondered if it had been hard for her, too, to imagine such a spectacle here, in this space which had been gradually overtaken by nature after its brutal desecration by men, in this land that despoiled all its temples. Could this photograph, like the dogs, be prehistoric?

When she was feeling less generous, Amma liked to tell me about the history of the refuge for girls and, more specifically, its early years, an era she called its "golden age". I sat on the ground, as I did every night, massaging her feet and her calves with coconut oil. She said, *April, you have such nice hands*, and she closed her eyes. She called me April because I had come in April. Each girl was named after the month she had been admitted to the refuge for girls and at times there might be a May-One, a June-Two, an October-Three and not a single December.

The refuge for girls had been set up by an American NGO thirty years earlier, when the population was fleeing the conflicts in the North and when men and women were walking on the roadside, carrying mattresses and pots on their heads.

Among these men and women were children without any relatives. *It was Pamela watching television at home in Wisconsin, do you know where Wisconsin is, April? She was watching television and she saw those children on their own and she said that if she could have climbed into the television and taken them into her arms, she would have. Oh, those white folks can be so stupid, they'll say nonsense like that! Pamela came here with a team and she bought this whole temple complex while the monks were still here. Some monks they were, they were drinking toddy on the sly and going to brothels, I'll have you know. Anyway, nobody wanted these sorry excuses for temples. You know, in the South, nobody wants to remember that the war had happened here, the people here like to say that in the South folks are too smart to fight, tsk tsk, they're so fast to forget, they'll frown when there's talk of Northern soldiers but back then there were soldiers here, too, destroying temples, waking people up in the middle of the night, burning their houses, kidnapping their boys and raping their girls! Pamela bought it all, had this building right here built, and that's how I came here. Oh, April, back then there were children coming in with bullet wounds, children who'd just stopped talking, not a single word, and then there were children who hadn't eaten in days, children who were half crazy and climbing trees like monkeys! Pamela brought in doctors, shrinks, she even brought in singers and clowns. Oh, that was really something to see, the refuge for girls back then! The children talked in English like the Americans.* Howareyouuuufiiiiiinethankiyouuuu. *Oh, what a nice team we made! We were even on television, that was the golden age of the refuge for girls, April, the golden age!* After

105

the golden age it was all downhill and Amma spoke as if it left a bitter taste in her mouth. *After that were the peace accords and then there were no more children to save. The doctors, the singers and the clowns left. Pamela stayed for a few more years and we saw ruined girls coming in whose families didn't know what to do with them. Like you. Or girls whose parents didn't care enough to try to keep them. Now, that's a crying shame, it is.* I wanted to talk to her about February who had lost her family when a bus blew up while she was at school, about June who saw her only brother snatched by men in ski masks and who was sure they were coming for her next, about June-Three whose family disappeared overnight, likely taken by soldiers, and who wanted to believe that they had lost their memories and were living a happy life somewhere out there. I wanted to talk to her about the safe and the pyre. I wanted to tell her that we were, all of us, children of an underhanded war that had supplanted the one she liked to tell me about with *ooh*s and *aah*s, that this one wasn't ravaging a whole country at once but rather sowing destruction little by little: in villages, by the rice fields, beside forests, at spots along the road, a blow here, an attack there. I had to guess that this sort of simmering, silent war with men who just picked up a weapon and then called themselves soldiers, with an army that lived deep in the forest like animals, this sort of war wouldn't show up on television in Wisconsin. But I wasn't about to say that to her.

I stayed as long as I could in the temple and when the sky turned pink, I slipped back into the building. I showered, I changed my clothes, I did my hair with my wet hands and I went to wake up the girls in the dormitory. There was always a minute in which the odour of dreams, of warm sheets, of tears and loss struck me at the dormitory door. It had been the same since the first day I lay down on the bed at the back. More than three years had gone by but I couldn't say what that meant, I couldn't guess what that amounted to. Were all these years a long path I continued to tread towards something that only kept receding further into the distance? Had something in me endured this stretch of time the way the temples' stones had weathered the decades? Had my heart hardened? Had my body been gradually worn down to the point of transparency, to the point of becoming indistinguishable from these walls? Might I wake up tomorrow as old as Amma, with a face creased by wrinkles? Three years, ten years, a thousand years, all were meaningless to me and yet, every morning, in the doorway of this dormitory, there was the distinct memory of what I had once been. I wondered where this memory was hidden, how it had remained untouched. It was there, right there, in this odour, and with it the three years were lifted like a veil. When I let it transport me, I saw myself in each sleeping girl, each one dreaming of something gentle and warm and caressing. All the faces were mine and in this multiplicity I had no way to escape myself.

I took down the gong and its mallet. One strike was enough to wake the girls; the truth was that I needed the gong just as much to assume my role, to shake off my memory. As they stood before their beds, their faces still clouded by sleep, I went to open the shutters. When I walked in front of them, they all, apart from the newcomers who didn't know the rules yet, said, *Hello Akka.* Sometimes I stayed silent and thought,

107

What's the point, because the day would be just like yesterday, just like the day before that, just like three years before.

We would spend the morning cleaning the three temples that still welcomed visitors. The floor had to be scrubbed, the courtyard swept, the garden tended to. Everything had to be spick and span when the refuge's gates opened to let through tourists. Some hotels set up lunches amid what remained of the temples, others used the rubble as a backdrop for photographs, and there was even the occasional film shoot. All the while, we had to be out of sight, invisible. In those stretches, we worked in the refuge's laundry room where the surrounding hotels' linens were washed. Sheets, towels, table-cloths – we swirled them in huge barrels of hot water then we scoured them on flat stones. Then they were put in dryers and in the afternoon we ironed them. Amma was very proud of her business; she insisted she would create a label called "Pampered by the Refuge for Girls".

I was no different from the other girls: I scrubbed, I swept, I planted, I scoured, I plunged my hands in near-boiling water and I scraped. Like them, I ate the same thing every day: yoghurt, rice, tomatoes and aubergine, bananas, rice, tomatoes and aubergine, coconuts. Like them, my hair was short, my brain nearly dead, my body stunted. But I was still their Akka who watched them, kept them from gossiping, day-dreaming, dawdling, whining. I struck them across the wrist with a bamboo stalk because if the work wasn't done, Amma would whip them herself, and with her there was no feinting, no holding back, no chance that one strike was enough. I was the one they came to when they bled and I told them what to do: I gave them rectangles of cloth and I showed them where to wash them. Some evenings, when they started telling their stories, I let them, despite knowing that was forbidden. The terrible whispers wafted from bed to bed, their sobs knit a blanket that they pulled up to their chins, and I stood outside but that was natural: I was their Akka – I'd scrubbed their bodies with that horrible gritty paste, I'd cut their long curly hair, I had no right to their blankets.

They didn't know that I hadn't burned their long plaits along with their belongings like I was supposed to. They didn't know that this vestige of their past life still existed, meticulously rolled up in a cloth, between two loose stone slabs in the old temple. When I disinfected my first girl and I cut her hair, she pleaded with me not to, she threw herself at my feet, naked, shaking. She was a March and one of her cousins came for her not long after. I didn't give her back her plait, it wasn't the least use to her anymore, but I liked thinking that my heart wasn't so cold and that, even when cornered, pushed to the brink, I still had a shred of goodwill.

I still burned clothes, shoes, photographs. I still gave the girls pills and that sticky black stuff. I saw what was in their underwear after, this mass, this form, which was both animal and vegetable, terrifying and fascinating. I saw how much they cried and I wondered each time if I'd shed such tears for this thing that I was told had made me a ruined girl.

Every so often, I don't know why, Amma decided to take me along on errands. She bought metres and metres of white cloth, medicine, rice, onions, garlic. I was always astonished by how loud and garish life outside was. I'd forgotten the way children laughed and played, I'd forgotten that women's fingernails could be painted and that men might have their shirts unbuttoned in front of us. In this walled city there were sellers on all the street corners and stalls on the pavement hawking everything. Fruits dripped from the displays and I had a feeling the yoghurt they sold in earthen pots wasn't even slightly curdled. I didn't care about this old-world scene, this hubbub, this chaos. Even though I knew better, what I cared about was trying to find my loved ones in the faces of each woman, each man, each boy. Sometimes a slight resemblance caught my eye in someone's mouth or posture or shoes or tone of voice or shirt or way of laughing but, no matter how hard I tried to summon them, they were never wholly there. Sometimes I caught the reflection of a young woman with short hair in a white skirt and blouse shuffling behind an old woman in a white sari. She looked back at me, waved at me, smiled at me.

There were six of us that November in the refuge for girls. All the girls who had been there when I'd arrived were gone. Some had been taken home again by their families, others were adopted, a few were sent away because the jelly and the pills hadn't worked, others still had left once they were old enough. It was a game of musical chairs I was now used to; ruined girls didn't stay at the refuge for long. With rare exceptions.

The girls queued up for the bathroom and nobody dawdled apart from November who had been there for a few days. She'd opened her mouth only once; the others insisted she was mute but I knew she didn't talk because she had no words left, just shrieks coating her throat. I knew that dazed look, those lips that bled from being chewed on, that stiff way of standing as if she were made of stone. When I'd cleaned her, disinfected her and washed her, she hadn't said a thing. When I'd cut her hair that had been long and in ringlets, she hadn't moved. She'd had to be pushed, pulled, shoved out of the way, told each thing multiple times. She often tripped, as if she had two left feet. When she ate, she didn't notice the food dripping down her chin. I didn't use the bamboo rod. I picked her up when she fell, I wiped her mouth, I brushed her hair for her when she couldn't. She was so thin that I could lift her up and set her in a corner where she stayed until I came back for her. I made her finish the banana given out in the afternoon and only then did I wave the bamboo in front of her, like a threat, but I think she knew I was bluffing because my face wasn't stern. In the evenings, she huddled under her blanket and I checked on her often to make sure that she was still breathing. I didn't know what had come over me.

All the girls were dressed alike in white skirts and blouses, and when we crossed the courtyard at a brisk pace for breakfast, I always glanced at Amma's office. Sometimes I had an odd impression of being in there again and looking out at that white flock passing by. Breakfast was eaten standing up: yoghurt and a bit of bread. No dawdling, I kept saying, *Let's go, let's go*. The night before, a group of tourists had had a celebration in one of the temples and there was no guessing what state they'd left the premises in. There was a photoshoot scheduled for noon in that same temple.

I assigned chores and kept November with me. I could tell

Amma was watching me closely and, to put on a good show, I scolded the other girls and pushed November in front of me so she'd move more quickly. We pulled weeds around a temple where all the sculptures along the wall had been beheaded. I thought I recognised the temple with apsaras, the one dedicated to the god of dance, from the photograph. I told November all these things, I didn't know why. Ever since she'd arrived, my thoughts had been like that: we'd be hunched down working, and they'd be like a song coming out of my mouth, telling of this and that and the other. We heaped up the weeds to be burned near the back of the courtyard. We had to make multiple trips, the stalks scraped our arms and we lingered in the temple for a minute after, stretched out on the cool ground.

November stayed at my side the whole day, she was my shadow, she kept bumping into me, she slowed me down. It should have bothered me, it should have earned her a strike of the bamboo rod, but I was touched by her unsteady presence.

In the evening, I went to see Amma in her office. I sat cross-legged to rub her feet and calves as if it were she who had spent the day working. That went on for ages – slather, rub, knead – and she didn't close her eyes, but instead she looked at me the same way she had the first day. Was she still reading my soul? When she asked me if the new girl was a good worker, I said she was a quick study.

When I came back to the dormitory, I couldn't take it any-more. The scratches up and down my arms were on fire, my fingers were swollen, the mothball odour of Amma's legs filled my nostrils. I showered, I pulled on my nightdress, I walked past each bed. Some girls were already asleep. No stories tonight, no tears either. November was under her blanket in a foetal position. She was breathing.

I lay down on my bed, my face against the wall. It was that time of night when I wanted to believe in God, any god, to believe in spirits and miracles. It was that time of night when I wanted to know how I should pray to a being who was somewhere above or below me, who watched over me and who I could beseech: make sleep come quickly.

I felt her hand on my shoulder and I didn't startle. Sometimes crying girls woke me up to tell me that they wanted to go back home, that they'd seen a ghost, or that they could hear their mother calling them. Sometimes the girls begged me to let them leave but I was their Akka, I couldn't do that, I led them back to their bed, and if they got panicky, I threatened them, I told them that I would strike them with the bamboo rod, that I would tell Amma, that if they didn't calm down there'd be even more work for them the next day.

I didn't move when November slipped into my bed. She pressed her body against mine, her breath on my nape, her arms clutching mine, her hand finding mine, and then our fingers interlocking. I felt tears come when her voice whispered, *My name is Tara.* I had known she wasn't mute.

13

By now, I should have learned not to get attached to anything or anybody. But that was obvious. Where, after all, was everyone I'd loved? Dead lost disappeared. Where was everything I'd learned, maths geography history biology physics Bharatanatyam, what use was any of that to me these days? No use at all. My father should have taught me how to swing a machete, my mother should have shown me how to be a sorceress and scare men, Aya should have shown me how to kill a chicken with my bare hands and make soup with wild herbs, Rada should have taught me martial arts, the boy should have spat at me and tamed me like the mean dog that I was, that was what would have been helpful for me now, that was what would have tempered me, made me a strong woman who could wield bamboo as she worked and watched, a *thwack* on the back, a *thwack* on the wrists.

I feared that the mind-numbing chores I performed day in day out would turn me not into the perfect Akka that Amma had hoped for – a heartless big sister watching tirelessly and burning plaits and crawling into the office each evening – but into a cold, indifferent Akka inured to life here amid the temples to no gods.

By now, this heart, this damned heart, should have known that it did no good to open itself up.

I was the only one to call her Tara and even though she asked for my name ten times twenty times I refused to tell her, I said, *Not right now, maybe later.* She had lived by the train station in the capital, she told me that her favourite thing to do after school had been to watch each carriage go by and guess what sorts of lives the people coming and going led. She mimed it all, her head turning this way and that. Her mother had embroidered fabrics, her father had been a taxi driver, and her two brothers had been students at school. She said that every Sunday her family would go to the cinema and with that she stood up, she mimed the actresses dancing and putting on airs. That got me laughing. We were hidden in the temple with apsaras, we snuck away for a while each day. I had once begun the Alarippu for her, that dance to honour gods and masters, but making it all the way to the end was impossible: my legs started wobbling, my teeth were soon clattering, and I collapsed in a heap. Tara stayed with me, not saying a word, until my breathing had calmed, her two hands pressed flat on my back. We ruined girls understood better than anyone else how language failed us when grief and loss grew overpowering. Each night, I slept with her against me and I didn't have to think up prayers, I didn't have to plead for sleep. When I woke up before everyone, she was already back in her own bed.

I didn't know how she had ended up here, so many

kilometres south of the capital, I didn't ask her anything, I noticed that, when she mentioned her mother, her left arm would start quivering and a vein would bulge on her forehead. Sometimes she jumped on me and hugged me so hard that I could barely breathe, other times she gently slipped her hand in mine and that was unspeakably sweet. Some nights, when I told her to go back to her own bed, when I pretended to scold her, she covered my face with small kisses *peck peck peck* until my insistence dissolved into giggles. I noticed how she charmed all the girls the minute she opened her mouth. Ever since her arrival, there had been a lightness in the dormitory that I'd never seen before. Tara mimed the actors from romantic comedies, smudged some chalk across her face to make a moustache and flirt with us, pantomimed kisses, fainting fits, starry-eyed women. She regaled us with descriptions of the trains, the peanut sellers who fought with the tea sellers who fought with the flower sellers, she play-acted the policemen who came to restore order and we doubled over laughing, our hands clapped over our mouths. I stayed in the doorway to make sure Amma wouldn't catch us and sometimes I sensed that the blanket knitted around the girls wasn't woven only with tears and that it was now starting to enfold me as well.

Our workload doubled in December and I didn't see daylight. The tourists, the rain, the stray dogs, the bats undid what we had done each morning. The hotels were packed and the bundles of dirty laundry piled up. We washed, we ironed, we sorted, we hardly ate, we could barely stay standing in the shower each evening. I slept in Amma's office and she sent me out with a merciless kick, calling me lazy. I reassured the girls, telling them that after New Year's Day, everything would be back to normal, that we just had to stay strong. They nodded, it felt like they had grown attached to me, that they trusted me, April, their Akka whose body was as worn out and whose head was as empty as theirs.

I knew it was Christmas Day because along with the bundles of dirty laundry came a basket of chocolates and fruits with a huge red card wishing "the team at the refuge" a very merry Christmas. Amma immediately confiscated it as we continued to work. The day was interminable, each second full to bursting with chores to be done. That day, even before nightfall, little green short-tailed parrots had been flying from tree to tree, letting out shrill cries. All the girls came out and we watched this ballet together. The green of the feathers stood out against the blue of the sky but as the sun set, the hues darkened and soon enough we could only hear them flying and calling out. Tara slipped her hand in mine and asked if the parrots had a language of their own. I recalled that, a long time ago, someone had told me that no language was above any other. I answered, *Yes, parrots absolutely have a language of their own.*

The basket of fruits and chocolates was in Amma's office. She hadn't touched it; the plastic and the red bow on the handle remained intact. As I rubbed her feet and she told me about the ideas she had for expanding the refuge's laundry services, I decided that I would steal this basket. It was odd how the thought came to me: so calmly, so decisively, to I, who acted like a slave here and who didn't dare contemplate going even a few metres to see the sea, not even when the gate was unattended. Was it because the day had been so gruelling? Was it because the basket was right there, like a precious, forbidden thing, untouched? Was it because I didn't want to let yet another Christmas Day go by like this, on my knees, sweating, my mouth dry with exhaustion? But maybe it wasn't so complicated as that. It was merely a wish to make my sisters happy tonight, to share a few simple pleasures the way so many families in this country were doing on this holiday night. Yes, I was going to steal it and I would deal with Amma's wrath. No thought had ever made me feel so alive.

It was easy. I had spent more than three years here, I might be dumb but I knew where each item belonged, I could pick out Amma's footsteps among all the others coming and going in the refuge for girls, I knew the sound of the gate opening for the van that brought the laundry, the groan of the dormitory door's hinges, I could distinguish the sound of the water pipe for the bathroom from that of the one for the kitchen, I knew which windows were kept open and the one in Amma's office always was.

The basket was there, in the same spot. Amma's mothball smell was still lingering in the air. I removed the bow, unwrapped the plastic, and emptied the contents into a sheet that I knotted tight. I read the card, and was about to slip it under my blouse, but then decided to leave it in plain sight on Amma's desk. I felt an uncontrollable urge to laugh at the thought of her coming in the next morning. I would have given anything for all the girls to see me right there and then, a girl sneaking around, snickering, unafraid.

That night in the dormitory, we doled out the chocolates. April-Two and June had never tasted such a thing in their life. I set out the fruits – there were mangoes, apples, bananas, passion fruits. Nobody wanted a banana. For a few minutes, the fruits and chocolates spread sweetness across our tongues and I could hardly believe that, a long time ago, every day of my life had been full of such deliciousness.

Tara crooned a Christmas tune she had learned at school. I knew it, too. My whole family had been accustomed to intoning it at midnight and, when she gestured for me to accompany her, I murmured the words. They were still so painful for me but, here, in this room that smelled like mould and grief, among these souls so much like my own, amid these bodies that had been through the same ordeals I had, I got all the way through them without wavering.

We tried not to make noise, we mumbled, we giggled under our breath when Tara began her performances, we kissed each other's cheeks, we hugged each other, we bit into our squares of chocolate and maybe, that night, I became a true big sister to them all.

When Tara slipped into my bed, I whispered my name at long last. *My name is Vijaya.* She repeated it several times, it felt nice to hear this name that meant victory, that name that my father had chosen. Tara hugged me tight, said, *Thank you for this wonderful Christmas present*, and I fell asleep without knowing whether she meant the chocolates or my name.

That night, I dreamed I was running, I was free, I was dancing. I was flying.

The next morning, as I was returning from the little

temple, already dressed, I heard Amma coming. I didn't stop, I wasn't afraid, I headed to the dormitory. She yelled, *April!* I took down the gong and struck it with the mallet several times, louder and louder. I started dancing, my head whipping back and forth, I jumped, I shrieked as if the time of the temples' splendour and the beheaded gods' glory were back in full force.

14

I was on my knees and the girls were facing me. Amma had
slapped me again and again so I would drop the gong. She had
asked me which of us had stolen the chocolates and fruits, and
I had said, *Only me.* She had asked who had eaten them, and
I had said, *Only me.* She had forced open my hand, closed it
over the handle of the bamboo rod, and told me to strike every
girl who knew that I had stolen the treats, who knew that I
had eaten them, and I had started whipping myself. Then Tara
had rushed over to me, shouting my name, my real name,
clinging to my neck, and she had said, *Me too, I stole, me too,
I ate.* Amma had stopped at that point and looked at us a long
while. She had torn Tara off me and thrown her to the other
girls as if she were just a twig. So there I was, on my knees,
facing the girls who were huddling together, holding hands,
holding Tara. They were all sobbing, they were pleading for
me, they were begging for Amma to give me another chance,
saying I wouldn't do it again. They promised to work twice
as hard. That was how I ended up in the dusty courtyard the
day after Christmas when in other houses, in other countries,

children were playing with their new presents. There I was, whipped but happy, my heart beating with something bigger than myself, feeling this sisterhood from head to toe, still hearing my own name in my ears. Amma took the girls into the dormitory and locked them inside. She hissed, *No food today for your friends*, put the key in her purse, and pulled me to my feet. What was she going to do with me?

She told me to change because my clothes were filthy. I only had one white sari left. I tried to read her face but her features were buried even deeper beneath her wrinkles than usual. She grabbed my arm and pulled me to the gate where we waited for the usual taxi we would take to run errands. I was surprised but didn't say anything. I had steeled myself, I was ready for any scolding or threats or punishment.

The taxi took us down the road through the palm trees and turned onto the main road. There were men in sarongs crouched down on the sand, maybe they were waiting until high tide to climb onto their stilts. Children were playing here and there on the rocky outcrops, were they looking for cowries to make necklaces they could sell to tourists? Were they catching red crabs in the stunningly clear water to boil for soup? Groups of women were already coming back from the market, their baskets overflowing with vegetables, it was the holidays after all. A bus stopped, full of young people who had come to spend the day in the old city where the alleys offered dark nooks for trysts. Life felt nothing short of radiant, did it seem that way because I had no fear, was it because the previous night's pleasures were still hot in my heart? It exploded in bursts of colours, flashes of voices. As we neared the city's old gate, the arch-shaped one, Amma told me she was going to send November back.

"Send Tara back?"

"Her name is November."

"But send her back to who?"

"To the person who found her on the train station platform. She was begging there, didn't you know that, April? No, of course you didn't, how could you know that when you're so stupid? You believe everything you're told. Do you know what happens to girls who beg on the streets?"

She grabbed my chin with a bony hand, forced me to look at her. She was whispering now, her sour breath enveloped my face like an old, damp rag. It was hard for me to breathe.

"They end up like you, they spread their legs for men and they like that. They end up like you. Ruined girls who are like dogs who let any male mount them and before long their belly's sticking out. You were lucky, though. You found me along the way – and this is how you thank me? You sneak around behind my back, you pull the girls along, you steal? How often do I have to say it, April? Nothing belongs to you here!"

I wanted to get out of the taxi but she had an iron grip. I wanted to run to the refuge, free the girls, take them with me, and run away, far away, and never come back. I wanted to hug Tara tight, tell her that life could be full of deliciousness, warmth, whirling, promise her all sorts of things. Deep down I felt something growing, a strength I didn't know I had but that I had seen before, long ago, in a smile before the darkness of the safe: an instinct that made me put up a fight, that made me kick Amma. I managed to get the car door

open, I fell forwards, the driver braked and shouted but not
because of me.

I was on my back. Above me, birds were flying as fast as
they could inland, they were crazed, they were fleeing en
masse. I stood up. All the cars had stopped, passengers were
getting out to look at the sea which was pulling back, it was
unbelievable, it seemed to be sucked up by something deep
in the middle of the water. There were children running after
it as if to catch it. Men and women were coming down the
pebble beach. For a long minute, there was no chatter, no
wind, no motor humming. Just the birds' shrieks.

I got up but Amma caught me, she dragged me to the taxi,
she was clutching my sari, my arm, and at that moment I saw
the crest of the wave. It looked like a steamroller of foam
barrelling towards us. There was nothing natural about it,
it was just like a machine. The world suddenly exploded in a
cacophony of noises, screams, groans, cracks. I broke into a
run but then

the water,

all this water

15

Something heavy trapped me in the water, I wondered if the taxi had flipped over on top of me, I had no hope of getting free but I struggled all the same. The next minute I was sucked in and spat back out, then pulled underwater again. How did I breathe all the while, was I possibly already dead? But then I wouldn't have been hurting so much. I felt my whole body contract then spread out, I flipped over, something was pressing into my belly, yes, I was at the bottom of all this water, I couldn't see anything. Something struck my shoulder and when I recognised my own voice screaming, I realised that my head was above the water. It was a black water, not the clear bright sea of this morning, it was something different, a monumental stinking blackhead that had burst in the middle of the sea and was now rushing outwards. I couldn't swim, I was being borne headlong, my feet were touching nothing, my hands were grabbing onto nothing. Other people went by, I could see their heads, I shouted, *Here, here, I'm here*, I held my arm out but they were doing the same thing, saying the same thing then disappearing. I caught hold of a tree trunk that had turned over on itself and I found myself underwater again, whirling, resurfacing, suffocating. I was whipped by branches, driftwood, I was still being borne along by the sheer force of the wave. Where exactly I had no idea, I didn't recognise anything, it could have been a marsh, it could have been a flooded rice field, but it couldn't be the sea.

Sometimes I was on my back despite myself and I struggled, I didn't like that, I wanted to see what was up ahead. Sometimes I managed to swim, I felt like the current had calmed but no sooner had I thought that than some new force bore me away. I tried in vain to grab onto all sorts of things, sheet metal, boards, shrubs, but they were like me, powerless against this wave. There was the huge wave and there were also what felt like rapid-fire waves whipping my face, submerging me, spitting me back out. I finally managed to clutch onto a branch, it seemed like nothing, I was sure I would be the one dragging it along, but it didn't give way. I used what little energy I had left to pull myself along it, my foot met a flat, hard surface. I climbed up even though the current was so violent I couldn't stand upright. Was it asphalt, was it a roof, I had no idea, there was no up or down anymore. I squeezed my eyes shut, I pressed my lips tight so as not to swallow the muddy water, I focused on my hands, needed them not to give out on me.

Whenever people went by, they looked like plastic toys floating in the water, bobbing up and down. They were small, light, insignificant in this morass pulling them towards something – but what could there be at the end: rapids, a huge hole? Anything was possible: the sea had exploded. I instinctively held my hand out to them even though they were metres and metres away, whether they were shouting for help or dead, face-down in the water. At one point I managed to pull up a little boy and a young girl. Their faces were caked with mud and I wanted to wipe it away tenderly and reassure them. When new waves slapped us, once twice three times, they finally let go of me, gently, without any struggle. I said, *Come back! Come back!* I sobbed and called to them as if I had known them forever and as if, without them, I wouldn't be able to live. They didn't look at me, they held on to one another tightly.

A little later, I heard a voice calling, *Help!* I looked up and I saw Amma clinging to a heap of branches. She got close to where I was, her wrinkled face contorted in a grimace, half her head bloodied, but she recognised me and started shaking, trying to climb up the trembling pile. She shouted, *April! April!* She held out her arm. I gripped my branch even harder, I recoiled. Amma tried to paddle towards me, *April!* She shouted in a threatening tone, but I didn't help her. She went by, her mouth opening and closing like a puppet's, and then she was gone.

I wondered what I would have done if she had found it in her heart to say my real name, if she hadn't threatened to send Tara back this morning, if she had thought to ask for help with a heart laid bare like mine and like those who knew that everything was long gone now, even ruined girls and the Ammas who slapped them.

The water ebbed and cries rose up everywhere. Haggard souls climbed out of all sorts of places, stumbling, getting back up, they walked without any idea of where to go. I managed to get down, I retched up muddy water, my mouth was full of sand, I felt like I had something stuck way up in my nostrils, by my forehead, I blew my nose, it didn't come out. I stuck a finger in my nose, twisted it around to try to catch it, but apart from sand and black lumps there was nothing and yet I could feel it, this thing scrabbling around and trying to get to my brain. I did my best to work out just where I was but nothing was recognisable. I was so close to losing my mind. What was this wasteland, where was the sea, where was the city, where were the fortified walls that had held out against so many armies a long time ago? Was I in another country? The sobs and shrieks grew louder. People holding others up, children dragging bodies along, women running with kids in tow, men trying to revive other men. People here and there called out to me because I was standing. They begged me to help find their mother, their father, their brother, their sister, their uncle, a car, they pleaded with me for water to drink, they asked me to watch their child but there was no child. I realised that these were words that came out of their mouths by sheer reflex, that these people weren't really talking to me, that they were speaking to a ghost in a dream, so I nodded and kept going.

I walked a long while along a river of slow-moving detritus. Sometimes I sank down to my knees, sometimes only my ankles had water lapping at them. I dragged my left leg, it was heavy and it hurt but I didn't want to stop and look at it. I'd lost my sari, my skirt was torn, my blouse wasn't buttoned over my front but I was unashamed. There were men and women naked and still walking just like me. Our bodies were covered in mud, leaves, vines. Our faces were filthy, our mouths dirty. I thought of Tara and the girls at the refuge. I had no doubt they were safe, locked up in the dormitory. It occurred to me that they might not even know about this wave at all; they might be sitting, worrying themselves sick, fretting over what Amma might be putting me through.

Amma. As soon as the thought formed, I batted it away. If I could have stomped on it and kicked it into the river of detritus, I would have.

I had to find my way back to the refuge, I had to tell the girls it was all over, I imagined Tara's hug, the way she would hold on to me like she was climbing a tree, I imagined all the questions I would have to answer, but first I would say, *Wait, I have something for you.* They would be impatient, they would be as excited as any girl who had been promised a surprise. I'd say, *Be patient, be patient,* they would follow me to my favourite corner of the refuge, they wouldn't want to go into this crumbling temple overrun by trees, they would be terrified that it might collapse on them. I would go in alone to my hiding spot to take out the parcel and I would give each girl back her plait and ask them to forgive me.

These thoughts kept me going and in this chaos, in this unfamiliar, apocalyptic landscape, as unlikely as it might seem, I imagined, with my sisters, a future, a better one.

I was sitting against a wall, I thought I had lost consciousness. A woman was wiping my face with a towel, she had me drink water that I spat out, it was black, sticky, it stank like shit. She had me drink more and more until what I spat out was clearer. I asked her where the refuge for girls was and she did just what I had earlier when people were asking me for help. She nodded. I asked her where the city was, she squinted and pointed behind her but I couldn't see a thing behind her. If the city was that way, then the sea had to be to my left and my back had to be to the refuge. I got moving again, my leg was so heavy, and this thing – a worm, an insect – in my head was fidgeting, I could feel it between my eyes, it wanted to get to my brain.

Sometimes I came across people whose clothes were dry and intact. They looked at me sadly, held my hand, they talked to me, but I shook my head no, I had to keep moving. A young boy draped a sheet over my shoulders and for a minute he kept his hands on me. He called me a big sister, too. He said, *Akka, there's a truck taking people to the hospital, come with me Akka, you're hurt.* His voice was so tender that I was about to give in, but I thought of my own sisters, I thought of Tara, and I pulled away. He didn't put up any fight. There were so many others to take to the hospital.

It was hot, the sun was high in the sky, how was that possible? Not so long ago, it had been morning. I recognised this bay, I recognised this low wall even if I didn't remember it being so black. The sea hadn't come up this far before. Had those coconut trees been bent over like that? Where was the path winding through the palm trees? Where were the palm trees? And yet this path felt oddly familiar to me, so I kept going, I turned here and turned there, I backtracked often. At one point, I was walking on huge red stone tiles, I wondered what they could be when suddenly it hit me. Those were the floors of the houses along the road! Everywhere I looked now, there were these squares with no walls, no roof, no furniture, no soul to come and take shelter in there, or eat, or sleep.

I couldn't say whether I had noticed the wall, the gate, or if it was the horde that led me to the refuge for girls. I refused to think about what it meant that the trees were on the ground, that the chairs, the driftwood, the metal sheets were piled up in the courtyard; I just looked at the huge temple which was still there, still standing, along with the others further off. They gleamed no less brilliantly than the first time I'd seen them. They shone under the midday sun, they were unbearably bright. I stepped over all sorts of things, I kept going, I wanted to get to the building at the end of the courtyard. There were men there, dry and intact. I told them that the girls were still there, I would show them, they had to follow me, but they were running this way and that, panicked, they didn't hear me. They were trying to clear away the courtyard by hand, how ridiculous to do that now, the girls had been locked up since this morning! They hadn't eaten a thing, they had to be terrified!

Afterwards, I would say that I didn't remember anything of that day. I would talk about the steamroller of foam and the branch I had clung to. I would say that I'd walked a long while, that I hadn't known where I was. Nobody would question my description of those weeks of insanity which so many other people couldn't remember any better, when they'd held tight to something, had marched for hours like zombies.

Of the building that housed the dormitory, the kitchen, the classroom, the showers, the office, Amma's room, all that remained was the floor, a long rectangle of polished concrete tile. How many times had I swept and washed this floor? I spun around, unable to believe that the steamroller of foam had barrelled so far inland and I tried to work out how many metres separated us from the ocean. A thousand metres? Two thousand? Dozens of people were circling around me, their figures indistinct as if time and space were warping, stretching out. They had no shadows, no faces, but their outlines left an impression in the air around me. I walked over to the bodies lined up further off, they were covered with white sheets, the same cloth that we cut for our skirts, our saris, our shawls. I looked at them, these were small bodies that had had far too little to eat and I wondered if all the people here thought, as I had thought more than three years earlier, that these were children. I counted them, they were all there, I tried to pick out Tara but it was impossible. Under their white shrouds, they were all the same.

A vehicle managed to get through. Some men headed over to the bodies and I walked up to carry one as well, I begged, they had no idea how much I needed to hold one, any one, tight in my arms. But they didn't hear me, they were in a hurry because they were scared of another wave. In the distance there was a siren and panic spread through everyone left standing. I heard the dull thuds of my sisters being tossed into the rubbish bin of the truck. A man tried to yank me along but I fought back so hard that he gave up. *The hospital*, that was all they were telling me. *The hospital, the hospital.*

There was only one place I could go now, the only place that could safeguard me, myself, my wounded body, my heart in shreds, my brain in tatters, my memory in pieces, my drowned recollections. I dragged myself to the little temple. Nobody seemed to notice. People were running away from the coast, afraid of it happening again. Could they be right? This time, I promised myself, I wouldn't hang onto anything, I wouldn't try to survive. The water had borne branches, clothes, bits of sheet metal into the temple. I lifted them up to get my parcel, the red cloth in which I'd kept the plaits.

Maybe in moments of great distress, in order to overcome what is beyond words, people like me create new prayers, new rituals. Maybe a long-buried memory re-emerges and turns them into witches, into sorceresses. I laid out five plaits, I christened them with the names of my sisters, I stroked them, I told them how beautiful they were. I danced for them, summoning up movements learned long ago that came back to me in fits and starts. I told them how we would live together and we wouldn't be afraid anymore, we wouldn't eat curdled yoghurt anymore. I cajoled them, I hugged them.

Could they maybe come back to life?

Maybe in this place that belonged to me in this small way, I was going mad. My dancing gave way to sobbing, I begged them to come back, I pleaded with them to forgive me. I saw the girls in this locked dormitory, watching the wave coming, unable to flee. If I hadn't stolen those chocolates, they wouldn't have been locked up. If I had been a true big sister, I wouldn't have put them in danger. I heard their shrieks of terror, I heard Tara calling out to me, and all the way to the end, to her dying breath and dying thought, she believed I would come and save her.

I threw myself to the ground by the wall. I did my best to relive their suffering. How I wish I could have been trapped with them, could have put an end to this dog's life! How I wish I could have protected Tara, small girl that she was, I could have swallowed her in one big gulp the way I swallowed all this water, all this shit, why had I clung to that branch? I called out to the wave and, just like before, I yelled, *Here, I'm here!*

16

In the haze, I sometimes heard a voice softly saying, *Tara, Tara*. I was floating in a cottony world where there was no pain, no tears. I could feel my body but it was like the darkness at night's end, both palpable and intangible, ethereal and present. My thoughts were round and soft, they floated from frangipani flowers to the taste of mangoes, they brought my mother's laugh to my throat and my father's hand to my back, they executed a delicate ballet in which the specks of memory never collided.

I wanted so badly to live that life.

I opened my eyes to this voice repeating, *Tara, Tara*. It was a white man whose eyes were the colour of the earth after rain. It wasn't my father but I liked seeing that colour as I emerged from this cocoon-like cottony haze. He repeated, *Tara*. He wasn't asking a question, he was just saying this name that I took in with deep breaths.

In that moment, my made-up life began. My second life.

The man's name was Emmanuel. He came to see me every day, he talked to me, he told me things about me.

He said:

Tara, someone brought you to a clinic, you really weren't in good shape, you were delirious, you were just saying your name over and over. They couldn't treat you there. Your shoulder was broken, your ribs were cracked, one of your lungs was punctured, you had a sinus infection, and there was a twenty-centimetre-long gash on your leg. When you got here, they wrote your name on the inside of your forearm in permanent marker, see, there's still a bit of it left.

He lifted my arm so I could see this name written in block letters. TARA.

Each day he gave me a little more:

Tara, you spent hours in the operating room, you had the whole team on tenterhooks with all your infections. You had the worst injuries of all but you hung in there, you got better. You've been in the hospital for a month now. I'm the one who stitched up your leg, I hope I did a good job. You can tell me once you're up and moving.

Sometimes he told me a little about himself:

I saw the pictures of the tsunami, I don't think I've ever seen such a sight. If I could have climbed into the television and come to help right away, I would have. I assembled a team and we got there on the twenty-ninth of December. You were brought in that day, Tara, you were my first patient.

In the room, others wounded came and went; nobody was a wreck like I was.

They thought I was relearning everything but the truth was that I was learning to live in this new body that had been broken, put back together, sewn up, this new body with a new name: how to breathe all the way in and all the way out, how to use my left arm to eat while my right shoulder was in a brace, how to walk again. Every bit of progress was another conquest over this skin, this flesh, these muscles, this mouth, this Tara.

Whenever the haze lifted, they came back to the fore: the plaits, the shrouds, Amma shrieking *April*, the taste of curdled yoghurt, the safe, the pyre, the boy, the girls, the feeling of the disinfectant paste biting into my skin. Then Emmanuel arrived, always: *Tara, shh, it's nothing,* he said as he had me swallow some medicine that brought back the soft, round thoughts. I wanted those thoughts forever, I didn't want anything else anymore.

I was wearing dresses again, I didn't care whether the patterns on them were flowers or shapes so long as they weren't white. My hair grew back and, one afternoon in the garden, I plucked a frangipani flower to tuck behind my ear. Emmanuel was no boy, he was a man with greying hair, crow's feet formed when he smiled, his smell wasn't minty but bittersweet. Even so, this man looked at me in a way nobody else did. He had this way of saying my name, I don't know what he put into this pair of syllables, but I wanted him to say it again and again, to make me believe in this Tara, the one he saw, the one he was bringing to life. He was a sculptor of sorts, shaping a body, chiselling a face, smoothing a madness, making this ruined girl into a woman full of promise.

I knew things about Emmanuel. He had been raising his son, Eli, alone since his wife had passed away. He had bought a flat recently. He had long believed he would never move on after losing his wife. It was the first time he'd been so far away from home, it was the first time he'd seen cane toads, it was the first time the smell of flowers had made his head spin. He was an innocent man who hadn't experienced violence and I wanted that virginity as well.

Nobody ever asked me anything but one day I described a life I had made up wholesale: a tapestry of lies, but a life I needed in order to survive, a life that wouldn't hold me back at every moment. A life where there was no mean dog nor gong nor bamboo rod, where I hadn't cut off plaits, burned photographs and scraps of flesh falling from girls. A life of warmth and deliciousness that was the imaginary extension of what I had experienced during my childhood, a life where I managed to swallow up Tara and where, deep down in myself, she was safe and sound and she lived anew, and blossomed, and staked out her territory. As she grew, she beat Vijaya back into a cranny and Vijaya let her, oh yes, that was all Vijaya wanted. I knew how grateful she, Vijaya, who had been abandoned by all, was for this respite. She had tried so hard for so long, had done the best she could. It was a relief for her to curl in on herself like a leaf as night falls. Tidily, quietly.

I said:

My name is Tara. I am twenty years old. My parents died in a fire when I was thirteen. I lived with my uncle and my aunt in a house with a red cement floor, a few hundred metres from the beach. The taxi we were in when the wave struck flipped over, I lost them. I clung to a branch, I walked for a long time but my house was gone, all that was left were the red cement tiles of the floor.

Emmanuel and the other doctors listened, nodding. They

didn't ask questions. I heard them talk about trauma and amnesia, about post-traumatic stress, I didn't know what those words meant but who was I to argue about what label to put on the mind of someone determined to survive?

A few days before he left, Emmanuel sat down beside me. He held my arm where the permanent marker was almost gone and he kissed me there, on the ghost of that name. He said that he would be back in a few months. He asked me if I knew what the name Tara meant, I shook my head.

He leaned in and said:

"Tara means many things: the guiding star, the liberator, the saviour, the conductor from the other side."

"The other side of what?"

"She ferries souls from ignorance to knowledge, from darkness to light, from grief to pleasure . . ."

"And from death to life, too?"

"Yes, Tara, from death to life, too."

In that moment, something came alive between the two of us. I had the feeling that he knew what was gnawing at my heart, that he could see me clearly, inside and out. I stood up and kissed him.

I remember that my mother had received visitors who wanted someone to love them forever, never to leave them. Those men asked her to fasten their hearts, I remember that odd phrase they used. Fasten their hearts. I had listened at the door and heard my mother say, *Are you absolutely sure? Do you truly want to be bound to this person for the rest of your life?* The men always answered, *Yes, please, fasten our hearts.* When my mother agreed to help them, she showed them what to do and, now, I rued not having listened to that part of the conversation because, as a child, I had only been interested in the men's problems and never in my mother's sorcery.

While my lips touched Emmanuel's, as my tongue sought his out, I thought of my mother. Wherever she might be, up above, down below, in this flower, in this bird, nowhere or everywhere, I asked her to fasten our hearts. I summoned her in this kiss, I asked her to bind me to this man for the rest of my life because I had a deep-rooted conviction that he alone could keep Tara alive, he alone could pacify Vijaya. In my mouth, there was a life in another country, far from this one, far from crumbling temples, pyres and ruined girls. On his tongue, I placed this new existence that I drew whole and without any cracks, an existence that he could sustain so long as he breathed. In his mouth a new family of three took shape: Emmanuel, Eli and Tara. In the tenderness and the force of this kiss, this family became mine. Soon I felt her, my mother, above us: sorceress, witch, moon-woman. She listened to me, her daughter, she understood me, she accepted, and for the final time, she said, *Yes, Vivi.*

ELI

The young man walks, his hand on the bulge of his messenger bag. On both sides of the path are strikingly yellow dandelions with stalks so long they can't stay upright. He remembers that Tara always kept pruning shears in her bag when they went on strolls and that, on the way back, she would cut whole armfuls. She would place the flowers in vases of all sizes throughout the flat, and scatter a few stalks on the windowsills too.

Eli has taken this path with Tara so, so many times, on foot or on bike, and, today, at dawn, he does not see anyone. The foliage seems especially dense, a heavy green, saturated with the chlorophyll that a full month's unrelenting rain has borne. He barely notices the wooden railway ties of the old tracks. As he steps off the path, he doesn't stop to take in the view. He doesn't notice that the meadows at the foot of the hill are still flooded. Eli keeps his head down, walks without letting himself be distracted, because he's still unsure what's driven him to come here. Something like that odd state of mind that sometimes arises – a spark, an instinct, an odd thought that lodges itself in one's heart, a compulsion. Yesterday, he scattered half the urn's ashes in the memorial garden, by those of his father, Emmanuel, who died four months earlier. The other half is with him today, in his bag.

On the span of the old railway bridge, he sits down. Between the banks, the water rushes onwards. In the distance, he notices the submerged roots of the weeping willow. He recalls how Tara always insisted on stopping here, going down to the bank, sitting under the weeping willow, lingering for a while. Here, she who was normally so timid, so reserved, would shout hellos to strangers with a steady smile. Might she have found, in this space suspended between two shores, a shred of innocence, a part of herself left behind in her homeland? What sorcery had been at work here, what beauty had touched her heart?

Eli stays put for a minute, trying to retain only the sound of the water, the sight of the sky crosshatched by the bridge's rust-red lattice, the feeling of the lush, rolling landscape around him. He pats the shirt pocket holding the ID found on Tara's body. It may only be a bit of plastic, but now this little thing will be one that helps give substance to his beloved ghosts.

Eli holds his breath for doubt or fear or guilt, but no such feelings overcome him here. His heart is at peace as the image of a woman who was discreet, loving and loved arises around him. Then he stands up and carefully pulls the urn out of his bag. He walks to the guardrail and tenderly, gently scatters the rest of Tara's ashes in the rushing water, in the very heart of this place she cherished, the same one where she decided to end it all. Then, between two diagonal struts, he hangs a garland of mango leaves tied the way she had shown him so many years before. Tara had told him that the garland was to bring luck, that the green leaves with aromatic sap were to ward off grief. Eli shuts his eyes, sees her holding steady the stepladder he had climbed, her face turned to his, her look both tender and worried. He hears her say, *Yes, it's perfect like that, Eli.*

Translator's Acknowledgements

With thanks to Katharina Bielenberg, Elise Williams, Rhian McKay and especially Allie Mayers for their magic at MacLehose; Frank Wynne for his encouragement; Allison Charette, Nell Freudenberger, Charlotte Mandell, Daisy Rockwell and Ahalya Satkunaratnam for their assistance on various regional particulars; Aqiil Gopee, Matthias Jambon-Puillet, Ariel Saramandi and Alex Valente for their advice on vocabulary; and of course Nathacha herself for entrusting me with her beautiful prose.